THE FOLKESTONE ANTHOLOGY
2014

FOLKESTONE WRITERS

THE FOLKESTONE ANTHOLOGY 2014

STORIES AND POEMS

EDITED BY JOHN SUSSAMS

Published by John Sussams
for Folkestone Writers
www.folkestonewriterspress.com

All copyright remains with the original authors.

All rights reserved. No part of this book may be reproduced or stored in an information retrieval system (other than for purposes of review) without prior written permission of the copyright holders

First edition November 2014

ISBN 978-0-9551952-5-9

To order additional copies of this book please contact the editor
(john@sussams.freeserve.co.uk)

Cover design John Sussams

Printed and bound by Parkers Design and Print
(team@parkersdesignprint.co.uk)

CONTENTS

A Matter of Pride	Colin Biddle	1
The Swan	Bob Brown	6
Dear Cecilia	Liz Brown	12
The Stalker	Helen Derry	22
A New Beginning	Angela Guidolin	28
Witness for the Defence	Margaret Harland-Suddes	34
Surfing off a Beach of Diamonds	Chris Holt	46
The Christmas Club	Helen Hudgell	52
Four Poems	Briony Kapoor	57
At the Bottom of the Stairs	Kate Jefford Lockwood	61
Just Another Day	Martin Posnett	67
The Orchestra of Attention	Peter Sharpe	73
Ferdie	Michele Sheldon	79
Friends and Strangers	Jacqueline Summer	84
Bureauphobia	John Sussams	91
What a Lovely Car	Barrie Thompson	97
The Tramp	Alexander Tulloch	100
The Hero	Alexander Tulloch	107
Ticket out of Poole	Mike Umbers	114
Flight	Mike Umbers	120
My Aunt Paddy	Britta von Zweigbergk	126

ABOUT THE AUTHORS **131**

A MATTER OF PRIDE

Colin Biddle

In the year nineteen fifty-one, when the aftermath of the Second World War still tried to smother pleasure out of day-to-day life in England, drabness remained the norm. He was eleven. That morning his mother received the letter telling of his failure to pass the Eleven Plus examination. His two brothers in earlier years had passed. A Secondary Modern School education beckoned. He'd been warned of what that meant. No chance to be a pilot or a doctor or anything exciting and uplifting − unlike his brothers − the world would open up for them.

He mounted his bike. Snow threatened. As it was a Sunday he didn't have to earn money picking Brussels sprouts on the Livingston's farm. When not at school he seemed to spend most of his time working on the farm. His summer holiday was taken up with spud bashing, not an easy job for an eleven year old. Ten shillings a day he was paid for over eight hours of work and as many potatoes as he could carry home in his shoulder bag while riding his bike. His mother needed the money and the potatoes, and carrots, and any other vegetables he and his brothers could nick under the nose of the farmer. Money was tight. After his mother had thrown his father out of the family home, his father stopped contributing to the family's upkeep. Potatoes in the shops cost a mint; so did carrots and Brussels sprouts. With what he and his brothers took from the farm at least they had plenty of what his mother called fill-up food to eat − not like some poor sods, his mother would say.

He'd admitted to himself long ago that he was the runt of the family. His brothers were bigger and stronger, not only because they were a year or two older, they had been so when of his age. They were smarter too. For some reason there were certain words he couldn't pronounce no matter how hard he tried, and that made him look pretty stupid. So did his excruciating shyness. He'd blush and have tears fill his eyes for the silliest of reasons. More like a girl than a boy, some said, making sure he heard.

He set off cycling towards the countryside with not only the bitter north wind making him sniffle and blink back tears. He didn't want to be a reject. This was what those attending the Secondary Modern School were called. He wanted to go on to better things which is what going to the Grammar School meant according to the headmaster of the Junior School he was now leaving. He wanted also to stay with his brothers, not to be cast adrift for that was what it felt like.

He passed through the village of Long Lawford, dismounting his bike for no particular reason at what locally was called The Meadow, the field which led to Tom Brown's Island. Hands in pockets, his shoulders hunched against the freezing wind, wiping his nose frequently on the sleeve of his duffle coat, he noted the fieldfares and redwings as he ambled to the bank of the River Avon at the point where the Sour Brook stream gurgled its way into it. The Sour Brook was always shallow. Even when swollen with days of persistent rain or a deluge, it never rose higher in depth than his knees.

Old Ned had foolishly entered the Sour Brook. Old Ned, a pike highly regarded by the local rod fishermen for its fighting ferocity and spirit. No one had caught it, yet Old Ned had been hooked many times but its violent thrashing, leaps, even somersaults, eventually broke all the fishing lines trying to hold it. That Old Ned would die of old age was the perceived wisdom of those who knew of these things .The notion occurred to him that catching Old Ned would earn him kudos. By nosing itself further upstream, even wriggling its silver body over a sandbank severely restricting the stream's flow, Old Ned seemed to be challenging him. He took up the challenge. Off came his duffle coat in spite of the cold, followed by his boots and long woolly, much darned, socks. He hadn't as yet been allowed to wear long trousers so his hand-me-down short ones could stay on. Gingerly he entered the water, squeaking as his toes pressed against the frozen stones on the Sour Brook's bed. Old Ned with difficulty swung round in the restricted area it dawdled in to eye him menacingly. Its long jaws rhythmically opened and shut revealing its rows of razor sharp teeth, an unmistakable warning to keep clear.

By biting his lip he strengthened his resolve to carry on in spite of the almost unbearable cold. On top of the sandbank he constructed a dam made from large stones, filling the gaps with pebbles but having the foresight to allow the water to trickle through gaps too small to be a means of escape for Old Ned. If he hadn't done this a comparatively deep pool would have quickly formed where Old Ned waited angrily swishing its tail. This would have increased the difficulties in coming to grips with the pike.

The dam finished, the battle commenced. He had no weapon other than his hands. Old Ned had its teeth, its spiky fins, slippery body and its whip of a tail. The boy's tactic was simple. Flip Old Ned out of the water and onto the bank. His groping, frozen hands were an easy target for Old Ned, as were his feet and ankles. Their first flurry of contact left him bleeding from a multitude of vicious bites, and Old Ned sulky. A second encounter followed, then a third and fourth. The daylight darkened, snow began to fall. This didn't deter the boy. He pressed on. He had a point to make and was determined to make it. "I won't give in," repeatedly he muttered. "I will succeed."

Old Ned's attacks became less ferocious and not so frequent. This encouraged the boy. Old Ned went into a defensive mode, trying harder to escape than to bite. Several times the boy managed to raise Old Ned out of the water only to lose his grip and so be unable to prevent the slippery fish from sliding down his pullover to fall back into the water. He was becoming soaked through by the snow and by the water he splashed up from the Sour Brook. The front of his pullover also became coated with a film of Old Ned's scales. Still the battle continued.

Not until the day was ending did the boy manage to flip Old Ned onto the bank. In awe mingled with a whiff of sadness he watched Old Ned perform its death throes. Old Ned had tested him to his limit. He'd won a worthy victory. What to do now? He had to take his trophy home to prove that he wasn't always a loser, that he'd started to leave childhood behind to become a man. But Old Ned even when dead didn't cooperate. Carrying the pike proved to be extremely difficult. Unable to take a firm grip, Old Ned kept slipping to the ground. The fish became coated with filth and snow. Still doggedly, the boy pressed on.

Foolishly he hadn't put under cover the clothes he'd taken off so they were as soaked as the rest of him. The cold bored into him with an intensity he hadn't experienced before. Carrying Old Ned while walking and shivering violently was frustratingly difficult. Carrying the fish while riding his bike proved to be impossible. Although the snow fell with increasing intensity, he wrapped Old Ned in his duffle coat, placed the duffle coat on his saddle and walked the four miles home pushing his bike. He knew his mother would fret over the lateness of the hour, the house rule being, to return home before dark, but he reasoned she'd immediately change her mood when he showed her what he'd done.

By the time he reached the back gate of his home it was very late, and he was extremely cold and wet. Hope she hasn't called the police, he thought, as he put his bike in the shed and carried Old Ned to the kitchen door. He'd started to cough in a way he hadn't coughed before. Only the pride of what he'd achieved stopped him from feeling wretched. He told himself he was on the way to becoming a man.

His mother greeted him with a hard slap across his face. She screamed on seeing the state he was in. She wasn't impressed by the now smelly, much battered, pike. It was disposed off without ceremony at the far end of the garden by one of his brothers. Dragged to the kitchen sink, there being no bathroom in the house, in spite of his half-hearted struggles and protests, his mother stripped him naked as though he were a four-year-old. Doing so shredded from him the maturity he thought he'd earned and so earnestly sought. After the two kettles had boiled (they seemed to take an age) his mother scrubbed him hard from head to toe. He felt too weak to resist. His hair washed and dried by vigorous rubbing with a number of towels by his mother, he sat in front of the coal fire, the only form of general heating, stacked with coal as high as was safe. Cup after cup of steaming soup he poured into himself. Two hot water bottles warmed his bed. Slipping between the sheets he felt feverish and more of a child than a man. If not a child, a Reject. He died of pneumonia.

---ooOoo---

THE SWAN

Bob Brown

Eduardo knew it would soon be time to make the decision. Feeling a little dizzy he instinctively breathed deeper to calm his pounding heart. Selena and Zachary's smouldering tango had electrified the ballroom leaving the atmosphere crackling with emotional static. Their impressive performance had exceeded even his demanding expectations. Eduardo was no stranger to excellence having taken many prizes himself at amateur level in his native Argentina – it was for this reason the Principal had begged him to judge the competition. Wistfully, he recalled his own college days in Buenos Aires when he had danced as if his life depended on it to win prestige or, perhaps, the heart of a blushing senorita. Even now, at forty, he still possessed much of his earlier panache which served him well in his role as lecturer at the university. He reminisced about how far he had come from the ghetto in which he had grown up. Desperate to claw his way out of poverty, it had taken all of his innate street cunning to forge his way ahead in the world. As a young adult he danced in bars for tips, learning both the art of tango and the ability to read people. The connections he made there helped him gain a scholarship in psychology. His fervent young mind was hungry to learn and he had studied psychoanalysis obsessively – a smart move in a city that was a world centre for psychiatry. However, his love of dance had never left him and, had he not graduated, he might have turned professional; a dream he still nurtured and partly the reason for his current dilemma.

Regaining his composure he glanced sideways at his fellow judges. One was the college bursar; he was there because the university had sponsored the competition. The other, Daphne, was an eccentric-looking retired ballerina who had once been quite famous. Traditionally, the university also supplied a professor of artistic temperament to sit on the panel and Eduardo, with his colourful history of Argentine tango, had been the natural choice. So impressive was his résumé of competitive dance that they made him head judge which also meant he had the casting vote in the event of a tie. There were three couples that had got through to the dance-off. First off had been the gorgeous Bianca and her partner, Gregio. They had delivered a sizzling Salsa which had left the audience baying for more. Eduardo knew Bianca well. She had joined his class two years ago as a fresher and they often came into close contact. He suspected she had a serious crush on him which he had not encouraged as, despite being sorely tempted, he did not want to compromise his position. Fraternising with students was frowned upon and might damage his career. However, at their last meeting, she had flirted outrageously; clearly signalling what was on offer should he seek her favours. This was part of his dilemma; he was attracted to her but was her youth and beauty enough of an incentive to cross the red line of college convention? Should he vote for her?

The second couple had been Selena and Zachary. Selena was a raven-haired temptress who could have been born to tango with her svelte frame and jet black eyes that could turn a man to stone. She was a very successful student at the university and her father, an important German industrialist, was a key provider of funding and overseas students. Knowing that her father doted on Selena's happiness, the Principal had left Eduardo in no doubt how displeased he would be if she did not do well; he had even intimated that next year's grant might be at stake. Eduardo hated politics when it came to dancing but knew what went on behind the scenes where power was concerned. As it turned out, Selena and Zachary's second dance had been good enough to win but voting for them would mean disappointing Bianca.

The final couple, Eve and Alistair, were just moving onto the dance floor. Daphne had enthused much about how they had *'captured the spirit of the dance'* in the first round. Eve was very tall and gangly and, with her short and simple hairstyle, was not as glamorous as her competitors. Her partner was a sensitive looking older man about twice her age, light of frame and slightly balding. He was a regular at the dance club and known to be a gentle and amiable soul. Their first round had been a sublime waltz and everyone had gasped at the mysterious chemistry generated by this innocuous looking couple as they moved through their routine. Eduardo was keen to see them dance again as an audacious idea had begun to take root in his mind which he wanted to develop further. As the lights dimmed he leaned forward in eager anticipation of the coming spectacle.

Overhead spotlights burst into deep shades of Manhattan blue whilst on the floor footlights cast opaque pools of silvery light. The effect was moonlight on a river. The violins of the introduction spiralled down into the melody as Sinatra's masculine baritone broke into the opening lines of 'Witchcraft'. At that moment, Eve and Alistair launched into a deliciously smooth foxtrot. Alistair's dance-frame was invincible as, with his back ramrod straight, he manoeuvred Eve around the floor with the precision of a maestro. Eduardo, however, only had eyes for the transformation that had overtaken Eve. Spellbound, he watched her float like a swan over the ground. It was indeed witchcraft for he could not perceive her feet ever leaving the floor. Gone was the plain, awkward looking girl of earlier; her place had been taken by an ethereal creature composed of sublime and effortless movement.

'She has turned in to a beautiful swan,' Eduardo thought, totally bewitched.

He shivered inside as he realised that Eve was no longer performing the foxtrot – she was the foxtrot! Sinatra's booming voice burst into his enraptured consciousness with the haunting refrain '**…arouse the need in me…**' and all too soon the lovely spell ended as the music died. The mystic swan became human again and her gallant dancing prince reverted to the kindly Alistair.

Eve's enchanted evolution from mere mortal to otherworldly being had captivated the audience who applauded thunderously. Eduardo instantly recognised the great opportunity such a power offered. His thrusting dream had always been to be the boy from the backstreets who made it to the big time and this was his golden chance. Eve's ability to become the *'spirit of the dance'* was beyond price; it was miraculous. With the combination of his dancing prowess and psychic skills he was sure he possessed the means of moulding Eve into the best tango dancer imaginable – she had the necessary basics, height and build, but it was the magic that she created that would propel them into superstardom. Using his obsessive drive for perfection he would tutor her relentlessly until, with him as her lead, they would conquer all before them; why, in Argentina they would make him a god! He worried not that she knew nothing of this plan or had yet to agree her part; all that could come later. If she could produce the magic with Alistair who was easily ten years his senior then she could do so with him. Capturing Eve would also capture her ability to enthral and with that kind of power he would make them both immortal.

The three women who were lining up before him each held a power that could determine his fate. Bianca offered the gift of love. In the past he had always been something of a 'Don Juan' but now could be the time to seek deeper love and he had a feeling she might be the special one. Selena offered the gift of patronage. He knew that she sought to excel in all things. He could feed this need by voting for her and, with the right words of carefully crafted praise, be sure to ingratiate himself with her adoring father. Voting for Selena would do him no harm at all. Eve offered the gift of magic which could bring him fame. Hers was the gift he coveted most of all but it came at a high price; it would cost him love or power. Also, there was the considerable risk that Eve might refuse his overtures and not want to become his protégé. She might reject him outright then all would be lost - dare he take the risk?

The Bursar chose Selena. Daphne chose Eve. His moment of truth had come; the one he chose would win for he had the casting vote. He looked at Bianca, the promise of sexual favour barely concealed in her expectant gaze. Selena eyed him coolly; in her mind she knew she held all the right cards. Eve was holding Alistair's hand tightly and gazing into his eyes for reassurance. Would she ever agree to become his dancing muse he wondered uncertainly?

He cleared his throat. 'The winners of the competition are … Eve and Alistair'.

Selena shot him a torturous glare of disbelief that seemed to say, 'You have betrayed me. I am the best.'

He wanted to look at Eve but he could not take his eyes from Bianca and watched as her sorrow welled up from somewhere deep inside to become a lonely tear trickling down her beautiful cheek.

'I did it all for you,' her look of heartbreak seemed to cry out.

Turning to Eve, he felt a cold triumph as he witnessed the look of grateful adoration with which she beheld the panel. Eduardo knew that his next challenge was to win her over to his cause and this he would do the moment the ceremonies were over.

As he made his way to the corridor by the changing rooms to wait for Eve he worked out a plan. A few words of congratulation followed by a celebratory drink; or even dinner. Once alone together he would use all of his Latin charm to impress upon her the brilliance of his strategies. Confident she would succumb to his genius, it would then be a short step back to Argentina and entry into the dance élite. At that moment his 'prize' appeared out of the shadows. They smiled sweetly at each other.

'Eve, you danced divinely, you fairly captured my heart,' Eduardo cooed.

'Thank you, Alistair was brilliant wasn't he?'

'Tell me, what is your magic secret?'

'My love is my inspiration.'

Eduardo was confused; what did she mean? He pushed on

regardless.

'You simply must permit me to take you somewhere special to celebrate, but first tell me, where did you learn to dance like that?'

'She learnt it from *me*!' rasped a deep husky voice behind him.

Spinning round he flinched to see Daphne, hand on hip, eyeing him suspiciously.

'And I will be the one taking her somewhere special. Are you ready darling?' Daphne enquired of Eve.

Eduardo watched crestfallen as Eve, with a playful little skip, rushed over to Daphne and kissed her openly. The pair gaily sped away lost in the thrall of each other's company.

He stayed in the corridor alone and desolate. He had given up the prospect of true love and ruined his career into the bargain – all in vain. Eve's magic had floated away; held in the power of another Svengali. He was defeated…

'Never mind Eduardo, if it's not too great a disappointment you could still take me somewhere special.'

He looked up to see Bianca, tears streaming down her lovely face.

'Whatever have I done?' he said brokenly, 'I wanted to control the gift of magic and all the time you offered me the most precious gift of all… love. Please forgive me Bianca'.

Bianca moved closer and tenderly took hold of his hands.

'Now Eduardo, I want you to teach *me* the tango'

---ooOoo---

DEAR CECILIA

Liz Brown

It was the slow passage of time – the mind numbing tedium – that really got him down. Why hadn't he foreseen the boredom? Now he could see the point of hobbies but what on earth was he interested in? For thirty years he had dreamt of retirement and when it arrived ten years early he could not believe his luck. Gerald remembered the day his boss, Kelvin, had called him into his office to deliver the news. His mind was sent into a frenzy of excitement. He, Gerald Underwood, would be master of his own destiny. Yippee! No more alarm clocks! Goodbye, 7.30am to London Bridge. He had never seen eye to eye with Kelvin but in that moment he could have kissed him.

Freedom had been great, at least for the first couple of weeks. He had spent more time with Sue until she accused him of getting under her feet. Bloody great! 30 years of sweating over a hot PC to keep a decent roof over her head and then she would rather volunteer in a charity shop than be his playmate.

Gerald looked down at the tiny clock on his computer screen. How could it only be 9.35 am? 30 years in front of a computer screen, watching the clock, wishing he could do something more with his life and here he was, money in the bank every month and what was he doing? Staring at a computer screen, that's what! He felt like screaming but what would be the use?

It was no good. A trip into town was called for; a nice cappuccino and an hour listening to the endless chatter of the young mothers in Starbucks. Whatever do women find to talk about? Well it was a mystery. Having eavesdropped, he couldn't see any point to their conversation but it seemed to make them laugh and smile. They were happy. Well he deserved a bit of pleasure – an almond croissant perhaps – to bridge the little gap before lunch. Yes, a walk into town and a little treat. That would break his mood. I'd better shut this down first, he thought, as his hand grasped the mouse.

'Ping'

Gerald saw *one unread email* chalked up on his Outlook Express screen. A despondent look crept over his face as he contemplated the likelihood of a *Groupon* deal on non-stick pans or cosmetic dentistry. However it could be a really funny joke or a video – the sort of thing that used to circulate around the office. That would cheer him up. He clicked on his inbox. Cecilia Jones. Yes, he had always been keen on her. Now she was worth a quick look. Cecilia was the type of girl who would make an excellent playmate. She would know how to have fun.

'Mmm, I thought they were back today,' he mused out loud as he glanced out of the window towards his neighbours' empty driveway. 'Well just one look and then it's off to the Starbucks kindergarten to tune in to the next incisive review of last night's Eastenders.'

From: CeciliaJ@hotmail.com
To:Gerald77@btinternet.com
Subject:REHelp
Date: Wed, 9 Oct 2013 9.38:07 +0000

Hi Gerald

I am really sorry to have to contact you about this. We are on holiday in Bermuda and have been robbed of all our money, credit cards, passports and return flight tickets. We are contacting you in the hope that you might be able to transfer some money to us to tide us over. We will obviously reimburse you when we are able to get back.

Best wishes

Cecilia

'Do they think I was born yesterday? It's obviously a scam. Well they can't fool me with this little charade.' Gerald was on the point of slamming shut his laptop when he had a change of heart. 'Well I do have a whole morning to kill and this could be fun. I'll show them who is boss around here. Let's see how they like to have their time wasted.'

Cecilia

It must all have been a dreadful shock. Hope you and Tom are unharmed. Yes of course I could let you have some money. How much do you need?

Gerald

'Ping'

Gerald

Thanks so much for replying straightaway. We are at our wits' end. Could you manage £750?

Cecilia

[end of message]

Cecilia

Please don't be shy. Is that enough? I could manage £1,000 and I guess it would help.

Gerald

'Ping'

Well if you are sure, that would be really welcome.

Cecilia x

[end of message]

Yes, fine. How do I get it to you?

G x

Gerald decided a tea break was in order and wandered into the kitchen to put the kettle on. The view from the window prompted memories of Cecilia sunbathing in her back garden. She was a sight for sore eyes - slim, blonde, all over tan, tiny bikini. Don't know why she bothered with it. She might as well have stripped down and given all of them a proper thrill. He was not the only man in the neighbourhood to fancy her and she knew it. He had put out a few signals - the odd wink here, an innuendo there. One Christmas, to his eternal shame, Gerald had tried it on with her after spiking her punch with a liberal splosh of Vodka. Even that didn't get him anywhere!

Settling back into his office chair, Gerald bit into his custard cream and let his imagination loose. If this were not a scam, how would it feel to rush in like a dashing hero to save the fair Cecilia, or to bend her to his evil will?

'Ping'

Gerald

We have spoken to our hotel and if you transfer the money to their account, they will let us have the cash. The details you need are attached.

Cecilia x

Gerald straightened up in his chair as indignation took hold. 'Oh yes that's really believable. Who do they think I am? How dare they think that I would be so gullible? Well they picked on the wrong victim here. I'll show them. We need to ramp this game up a few levels.'

Cecilia

I have been considering my position here. What's in it for me? If I help out, am I on a promise when you get back?

G x

'Ping'

Gerald

Whatever do you mean?

Cecilia

[end of message]

Don't be coy. You know how I feel about you and it's not as if you haven't encouraged me. I know the signs.

G x

'Ping'

Gerald

I am sorry but I don't recall leading you on. We are in a stressful situation here. Please don't be unkind.

Cecilia

[end of message]

Cecilia

You must remember getting plastered at last year's Christmas party. Don't you remember what you were doing when Tom almost barged in on us?

Gerald x

'Ping'

Gerald

Look I was a bit tipsy and I don't quite remember. Please don't embarrass me.

Cecilia x

[end of message]

Cecilia

In vino veritas!

Well you certainly were a little tigress that evening and that's no mistake. Tom's a lucky chap if you are half as enthusiastic with him. Don't you remember grappling with my trousers just as he walked in. If it hadn't been for my quick thinking dive to the ground, in a feigned attempt to find my contact lens, all hell might have broken loose!

Gerald x

'Ping'

Gerald

I am sure that's not true.

Cecilia

[end of message]

Cecilia

Well if you don't remember that, what about the practically nude sunbathing in your back garden, while Tom is out of the way? You don't give the impression of being a shrinking violet. And I am not the only red blooded male who has noticed your all-over tan! Then there is the ostentatious pampas grass display in your front porch. Doesn't everyone, save the most naïve, recognise that as a sure signal that you and Tom are a couple of swingers? Is that where you two disappear to every Saturday night while I have to sit through another episode of 'Strictly Come Dancing'? If you want to have fun, why not swing over in my direction for a change?

£1,000 is a lot of money. If I am good enough to be your friend in need, I think it's only fair that I get a favour in return!

G x

'Ping'

Gerald

Ok. Let's sort it out when we get back. In the meantime, please transfer the money.

Cx

[end of message]

You don't get away that easily. A promise or nothing!

Now Tom's snooker night is Friday week which will coincide very nicely with Sue's evening out with the girls. I suggest I stroll over to your place, with a bottle of something rather special under my arm, and we carry on where we left off last Christmas. And if you could wear that tiny red baby doll set I have seen fluttering on your washing line in recent months, all the better.

G x

'Ping'

OK

Cx

Gerald lolled back again in his chair. 'Well I think I can take that as a triumph,' he exclaimed, slapping his hand on the desk in an affirmation of his manly conquest. 'That scammer did me a favour. It's done my blood pressure no end of good to get that little lot off my chest. Now, first things first, I'd better make quite sure there's no evidence.' Gerald deleted the string of emails and emptied his 'deleted' folder before closing the lid on his lap top. It's a bit late for a coffee, he thought to himself as he grabbed his coat and so he walked off down the drive in anticipation of a pint and a steak pie at the 'Clarendon'

The afternoon sped by splendidly and Gerald was looking forward to a nice snooze in front of the TV as he turned his key in the front door lock at 6.30pm.

'Hi Gerald, is that you?' Sue called out from the lounge. 'I have invited Tom and Cecilia in for drinks. We were just wondering where you were.'

Gerald felt a pang of guilt as Cecilia stood up and kissed him on both cheeks. 'I had a slightly worrying email this morning but guessed it was a scam.'

'Yes, sorry about that,' muttered Tom. We're not sure how many of Cecilia's friends received it. Anyway, no harm done and the police are forwarding the emails.'

'Oh,' whispered Gerald under his breath.

'I'll get the drinks and you can tell us all about your holiday,' said Sue en route to the kitchen.

'I tell you what, let's fire up the I-pad and show you the holiday snaps,' enthused Tom, already making himself at home on Gerald's favourite armchair. 'Cecilia, your emails are stacking up here. There are over 40 of them. Can you believe it? Well Anne was well and truly taken in, poor thing. You had better call her and let her know you are safe. Why are women so gullible Gerald? At least you didn't fall for it. And now there's Carole. I have always thought she was a bit batty but this email confirms it!' Tom chuckled.

'Well what's the joke?' Sue enquired as she placed the drinks tray on the coffee table. 'I'll just go back for the nibbles - then you can tell me.'

'What's the problem, you....' Before Cecilia could finish, Tom jumped to his feet and pulled Gerald up by his collar. Cecilia's bloodcurdling scream brought Sue hurtling in from the kitchen, only to witness Tom frogmarching Cecilia out into the night, slamming the front door behind him.

'What on earth did you say to them?' screeched Sue, carving knife in hand.

Gerald slumped back onto the sofa. His trembling hand rattled the ice cubes in his empty glass. 'I'll tell you but first we need a refill and you had better put that knife down.'

---ooOoo---

THE STALKER

Helen Derry

A fierce wind whipped the delicate garments into a dancing frenzy as Mandy struggled to release them from the line. She detached the last pair of lacy briefs and sprinted across the lawn into the kitchen as the sky darkened and the sleet began in earnest.

She ran her fingers through her wind-blown auburn hair. Humming, she patted her spaniel, Meg, and dropped the little pile of underwear on the kitchen table and put the kettle on to make herself a cup of tea. While she waited for it to boil she began to fold the nearly-dry bras and matching briefs. Suddenly she stopped puzzled. Her eyes widened as she stared at the remaining black bra and pink thong.

She rushed out in the driving sleet and hunted frantically on the ground under the washing line. Nothing. She searched all over the lawn and neat borders. Nothing. Casting a nervous glance over her shoulder she ran into the kitchen, immediately locking the back door and shooting the bolt. She dragged the check curtains together and sank shivering onto a kitchen chair.

It was starting all over again. He was out there, watching her. She knew he was. She switched the kitchen light off and waited until her eyes became accustomed to the twilight. Her hand shaking, she stood to the side of the window and pulled the edge of the curtain back a fraction until she could see out into the darkening garden. A mistle thrush was singing in the apple tree. She peered slowly round, willing there to be no one there. The garden was empty. Gradually her eyes adapted to the poor light and she looked across the hedge to the cornfield beyond. Suddenly the last rays of the setting sun reflected off a metal object and to her despair she made out a pair of binoculars held by a thick-set man in a dark hooded parka.

He was back.

She dropped the curtain and stared at the phone. Her long wet hair dripped into her eyes and her fine cotton blouse clung to her skin but she could not force herself to go upstairs and change into warm, dry clothes. Not until the phone had rung. It would ring. She knew it would. It always had. But there was a silence which reached out to her, soothing her pounding heart into its usual steady beat. She breathed deeply into the silence and her muscles relaxed. Meg whined and licked her hand.

Finally, she crossed to the Aga and reaching for the familiar blackened kettle she poured herself a cup of herbal tea, glancing behind her at the phone. She sat in the grandfather chair, placing her tea on the scrubbed pine table, and thought. The poor light must have played tricks with her eyes. The farmers often strung old cd's up to scare the birds. That must have been it. No binoculars, no man. He would have rung by now. He always did.

She refused to name him even in her thoughts. That would give him power and destroy these last few blessed months she had been free of him. Judge Redmayne had granted her a six month injunction but refused to extend it further despite her barrister's eloquent plea that the petty officer presented a very real danger to her client. The judge was a great believer in human rights and said he could not curb a man's freedom. She had wanted to scream,

"What about a woman's freedom?"

Mandy finished her tea and, placing her cup on the draining board, pushed open the oak door and climbed the steep stairs towards the bathroom. Dropping her clothes in a sodden heap, she stood under the hot stream of water, warmth returning to her stiff limbs. And then she heard it. A faint ring. Steeling herself to ignore it, she massaged shampoo into her hair. She would not answer him.

Then the answer phone clicked in and she heard her mother's pleasant voice asking her to ring back. Smiling with relief, she rinsed her hair and wrapped herself in warm soft towels. She padded through to her bedroom humming a melody she had heard on Classic FM and drew the cream silk curtains, head averted from the garden. Towelling her thick hair dry, she slipped into a clean pair of jeans and an Aran sweater. Making herself comfortable on the bed she reached for the phone.

"Hello, Mum. How are things? Sorry I missed your call. I got soaked and had to shower."

"Mandy, lovely to hear your voice. But you do sound a bit odd though. Everything ok, darling? I know that your injunction expired today and I was worried that that monster would try to contact you."

Mandy paused. Her mother didn't miss a trick. But she wasn't going to scare her. Not yet. Her parents had suffered enough.

"I'm fine, mum. He hasn't been in touch. I don't think he'd risk another court appearance. This awful weather is getting me down: sleet, high winds and storms. I'm fed up with it. I can't wait for the spring. I've been flicking through travel brochures. Morocco seems very attractive at the moment with its sun, sand and souks."

Mandy smiled brightly as she spoke to make herself sound more enthusiastic than she felt. She could hear her mother thinking.

"Who would you go with now that you and Michael……"

Her voice trailed off. Mandy rescued her.

"Since Michael and I got divorced you mean. It's alright, mum. You can use the D word. It was a year ago and I've moved on."

Like hell I have. Lies seemed to trip off my tongue these days, she thought. Deceiving your own mother is a stupid thing to do.

"I'm sorry, Mandy, but it still upsets me. He was a lovely man and I thought he'd stick by you."

"Well he didn't, did he?"

Mandy almost shouted, but regretted it seconds later.

"I'm sorry, mum. I didn't mean to get upset. Tell you what, I'll ring you tomorrow. I've got to dry my hair and cook a bit of supper."

"You would tell me if there was anything wrong, wouldn't you?"

"Of course. Don't fuss so. I'm not a child."

They parted on fragile terms and Mandy almost wished she'd told her mother how scared she was that it was starting all over again. She needed comforting but wasn't selfish enough to burden her mother. Especially if it was a false alarm.

The shrill ring of the phone cut through the high pitched drone of the hairdryer. She switched off and waited, a strand of hair in her hand. She stared at the phone and then realised it was probably her mother ringing back to make it up. She picked it up.

That awful familiar pause and then it started. The heavy breathing, then the silences. She slammed the phone down as though it was red hot. It rang again and she picked it up and left it off the hook. The answer phone cut in and after the beep there was a nasty laugh. She held her breath, eyes screwed shut, and waited.

"You're holding your breath and closing your eyes, aren't you, my love? You see, I know you inside out: what perfume you wear, what music you listen to on Classic FM, and, most of all … your taste in underwear."

She shuddered wrapping her arms around herself. His Geordie accent thickened as he continued.

"Quite the little tart, aren't we? Cream lace, pink thongs, black sheer hold-ups with those sexy seams. You know what turns a man, don't you, my love? You pretended to be a little Puritan, faithful to that boring prig of a husband, didn't you? But I know better. You're hot. Red hot. You little tease."

His breathing between sentences came in gasps. Tears spilled down her cheeks at the humiliation. No longer able to stand his taunts, she seized the phone.

"Leave me alone! I never gave you any encouragement. We were just colleagues. I loved Michael, and you drove him away. You ruined my life with your obsession."

He snarled, "And you ruined mine with your false accusations. Got me drummed out when all I'd ever wanted was to join the navy. Sleeping with most of the tribunal, weren't you? You lured me in with your green witch's eyes and the way you wiggled across the mess in your uniform, you little bitch. Michael's well shot of you."

"How dare you talk about him," she screamed.

"Oh I dare. I'm going to show you what I think of your injunction and the lies you told to the court. But the judge wasn't impressed, was he? And now, I'm going to tan your backside with my bare hand and hold a knife to your pretty face. Then you won't be so high and mighty. You'll f--- me to stop me slicing you and then you'll beg for more."

He panted and she slammed the phone down and clasped her hands over her ears. She had never even been on a date with this psychopath and certainly not slept with him but he had convinced himself that she was his. She lay on the floor curled up in a foetal position, hands clenched, and waited for the phone to ring again. As she lay there frozen with fear, the silence stretched out and she began to hope. He had given up. Her hatred had finally penetrated his shell. She took deep breaths as her counsellor had told her. Calm, peace, relaxation.

And then she heard a faint scratching at the kitchen window downstairs. She switched off the bedroom light and shrank against the rough wall refusing to consider that it might be him. She tried to convince herself that the Virginia Creeper had blown loose in the gale and was whipping against the window. Then Meg growled, a low menacing growl.

Mandy forced herself to creep down the steep stairs. Feeling her way along the kitchen wall she searched about until her fingers made contact with the knife block and she selected the carver. She was trembling with fear but determined to defend herself.

She heard a scraping as though a blade was being run down the window frame. It was only a matter of time before he opened the old window. Meg growled again and looked at Mandy. The scratching became more frenzied and then there was silence followed by a loud crash as the glass shattered and a stone thudded onto the quarry-tiled floor. An arm reached in for the catch and Mandy rushed forward.

She lashed out blindly with the carving knife as Meg seized the sleeve. The arm tried to withdraw but Meg clung on with bared teeth and by now Mandy was beyond caring. She slashed at the fingers and heard an agonised scream. A white face loomed out of the darkness with staring eyes. Then, with a tearing sound he was gone into the night.

Shaking, Mandy staggered over to the light switch and blinked at the sudden brightness. Her eyes were drawn to the jagged window and the torn material flapping there. The outside security lights had come on and the garden was empty. She watched the washing line thrashing in the gale force wind.

She looked down at the knife in her hand, its blade wet with blood. Her eyes were drawn onwards to Meg who was sniffing at an object on the tiled floor. She knelt down and reached out to pick it up but realised to her horror that it was a finger. Her stalker's finger.

And then the phone rang.

---ooOoo---

A NEW BEGINNING

Angela Guidolin

Sahasra woke up sobbing, and feeling her face wet with tears, when she heard her beloved husband Bitasok's soft footfall in their modest bedroom. From the street, noises of stalls being assembled and of cars passing by pierced her ears, while the mixed aroma of curry and coffee assaulted her nostrils.

"Another bad dream?" Bitasok enquired gently, sitting by her in the dim light and wiping away her wrinkle-free face with his smooth hand. She sniffed, then nodded, her throat so tight that it hurt. She rolled toward him, pulling her knees up toward her chest, trying not to weep. He sighed and shook his head, caressing her long, straight hair.

She sniffed again and looked at him. "Why don't you just hug me? Why don't you kiss me?" She longed to ask him. Instead, she replied, regaining her composure,

"This time I was in this medical lab where I felt at ease, as if I had been spending plenty of time there. The light was on and the blinds were down. I was sitting on an armchair, checking my watch every few minutes. It was around eight and I was worried you wouldn't come. I knew I had better review the final steps of the procedure once more, but I felt my hands sweaty and shaky, and I found it hard to concentrate. As time went by, my breath became more and more shallow and my body was shaken by tremors. When you joined me at last, it was half an hour later. You apologised, blaming some colleagues who wanted to celebrate an amazing profit they had made at the Stock Exchange that day."

Sahasra paused to blow her nose and remember more of the dream. "You brought me strawberries, which you had bought from my favourite shop, on your way home. You called me Surina, and said that my new name, Sahasra, was beautiful and very appropriate, because it means 'new beginning'. You said that you were happy to leave Mumbai. You were tired of selling your soul every day, that a career change was in order, and Calcutta seemed as good a place as any to start from scratch. And that you would get used to your new name, Bitasok, 'One who does not mourn', because that is exactly what you planned to do."

Sahasra breathed deeply to steady her breaking voice, her sore eyes closed. "But I kept on calling you Anurag, and asked you to call me Surina. I told you that I hoped you and Sahasra would have a long and happy life together; that I had performed my memory tranfer to the best of my ability, but that this was still a highly experimental procedure; that there could be glitches you would have to fix, and that it was important to go through the troubleshooting techniques again, before saying farewell.

Sahasra halted to recall the rest of the dream, and realised that Bitasok had stopped caressing her. He had stood up, switched the light on and was getting dressed, his movements quick but clumsy at times, his eyes focused on the task at hand. A little resentful of his sudden change of attitude, she continued, watching him putting on his pure white loose tracksuit top and raising her melodious voice. "But you convinced me to taste the strawberries. They were so so sweet and juicy, like life itself…" Sahasra shivered. "You know, I haven't had strawberries for as long as I remember, because the mere sight of them distresses me. I wonder whether they taste the same way in reality. Maybe one day I'll muster enough courage to find out … Anyway, after we savoured them, you started to kiss me all over, and undress me slowly, saying that you didn't want to waste our last hours together, that you were scared too, and that you had agreed to my crazy plan out of love for me. That my last hours should be filled with joy and not fear − the fear you read in my eyes.

I could feel your warm and delicate touch on my skinny and failing body. I was not ashamed of it any more, because you made me feel beautiful. In the heat of the moment, we banged against a few monitors and keyboards, till we lay down on a huge examination table. From then on the dream becomes weirder, because it's as if I was split into two people. I was Surina making love to you as Anurag, and I was Sahasra next to you two, under a sheet on the same cold examination table. How could I be two people at the same time? Under the white sheet, I opened my eyes and gradually moved the arm that was farther away from you up to the edge of the bed. I wanted to leave the room without you noticing me, but I didn't make it. Suddenly Surina exhaled her last breath, and I felt a surge of despair. That's when I woke up."

Bitasok had finished putting on his clothes. "Can we talk about it tonight?" he asked her, leaving the room.

"No, there is no need. I'll book an appointment with a psychologist today. Waking up every morning like this is unbearable. And I feel that this dream completes the picture given me by the previous ones. I am afraid that I will wake up every morning with this acute sense of loss, if I don't find out what my subconscious is trying to tell me."

"No need to see a phychologist. You'll be fine."

"Maybe *you* can help me. Your students tell me all the time what a wonderful meditation teacher you are."

"Maybe. Now, think of something nice and you'll be OK. Tomorrow it's your big day. You'll start to teach singing in the poshest college of Calcutta. It's your first job after your memory loss a year ago! Shop for new clothes. See you at lunchtime," Bitasok added in a raised voice, while doing up his old trainers' laces and picking up his house keys from the carved wooden bowl by the entrance door of their small flat.

"Oh please! I can't! The feelings are too powerful! I wish there were an off switch in my mind! I've been unable to meditate for a long time now." With quick steps, Sahasra reached her husband before continuing. " Whenever I try, I seem to relive a past life, somehow connected to this dream. I know I was Surina in that life, and always lived in Mumbai. But maybe I should call it parallel life, because the experiences I recall involve mobile phones, TV programmes, computers and scientific labs!" She shrugged her shoulders and stared at him. "Or it is my mind that has created this Surina?" Sahasra wondered. "But how? The feelings are so authentic! And her experiences… so different from mine, although we both love singing, and music, and you, or Anurag. They had such a deep relationship, full of passion, intimacy, and understanding…" Her voice trailed off. Bitasok stood opposite her, as sympathetic as a lamppost.

"Actually, I began to have these parallel life flashbacks a few months ago, after hearing you calling Surina in your sleep!"

Bitasok raised his eyebrows, his lips slightly apart. "Well, who is she then? What's going on? "Bitasok's face turned as white as his top.

"That's it. I'm leaving you." Sahasra stated in a flat voice, but waving her hands furiously."Basta! You don't care about me anymore! You don't even want to have sex with me! I repulse you! Don't deny it! I see it in your eyes every time I try to seduce you!"

"You can't leave me."

"Give me one reason to stay. One!"
Bitasok replied deadpan, shaking his head, "You need me."

"No, I don't!"

Wearing a placatory smile, he reached out to her, and brought her small, black-haired head against his chest. "I know where the off switch is located." Betasok whispered in her left ear.

"Surina was my beloved wife. When she knew she was going to die of a rare disease, she built you and transferred her best memories to you. After her funeral, I left Mumbai and started a new life here in Cacutta. When I was ready, a year ago, I activated you. Only… You are right, you repulse me. You and your smell of expensive perfume. You and your flawless skin. You and your selfish personality. You and your still completely dark hair!"

His breath was warm on her left ear, his arms strong around her neck and shoulders, his right hand grasping and releasing locks of her hair, faster and faster, as if seeking something on her scalp and time was running out. With her right ear, Sahasra heard Bitasok's heart beating wildy, but not as fast as hers. She was afraid it would explode, killing her even before her husband tried. She could move her left leg.

"I don't understand. You don't talk any sense. Let me go, my neck is aching. " Sahasra mumbled in a thin voice. *If he doesn't release me, I'll tread on his toes*, she thought.

He stopped tousling her hair, and his big, steely right hand pushed her head firmly against his chest. *Now*! But her leg did not move. Her arms were paralysed. Bitasok lowered his arms slowly.

"I can't move! I can't feel my body! Call a doctor!"

In a warm tone, gazing at the empty wall of the corridor and standing still, he whispered, "Surina was a true woman! Her skin felt rough around her knees. She had a few wrinkles around her intense eyes, and I could still see the effect of the acid she had received on her face by her father for having fallen pregnant by me when she was fifteen."

Bisatok kept quiet for a few minutes, in a dreamlike state, ignoring Sahasra's requests for help. "How I miss her whole-hearted laughs! How I miss her aging body! How I miss her insecurity, her generosity, her rage toward injustice, her desire to be compassionate toward her parents and her inability to do so. She was on my side when I lost my highly paid job at the bank, and I was at the brink of depression. And when my parents died in a car crash. How I miss you !"

Desparation dripped from his voice. Sahasra felt a pang in her heart. She knew he was telling the truth, and yet she had been the only woman in his life.

"I'm sorry for your loss, but please help me." she begged, playing along. "I couln't give her the thing she wanted most in life: a child of our own. So when she told me about you, I thought it was the least I could do for her."

He paused, then addressed Sahasra. "She told me that if she

transferred to you only her best memories, you would find it easier to be a more loving and lovable person. The truth is that without remembering also her failings and dilemmas, you are as shallow and interesting as a puddle. I guess she also wanted an unencumbered new beginning, an easier second chance..."

"I don't understand a thing. Please, call a doctor!"

Bisatok carried on, lost in his thoughts, 'Surina is gone for good, and so should you.'

"You are Anurag! My dreams, my flashbacks…it's all real then!" she screamed, connecting the dots.

"Yes. Something happened that night that enabled the transfer of Surina's last memories. It was not supposed to happen. I'm sorry, but I cannot live with you. And you cannot live without me. I'm the only one who can fix the glitches."

The switch was at the base of her left ear, under her grown skin. He pushed it, and found himself lulling a rigid, lifeless android, tears rolling down his cheeks.

---ooOoo---

WITNESS FOR THE DEFENCE

Margaret Harland-Suddes

A Dramatic Narrative for four voices.
Characters: Narrator; Defendant; Witness; Judge.

NARRATOR
The days of the trial were ending. Only one Defence witness to hear.
The courtroom was electric with tension waiting for the judge to appear.
With stumbling steps the defendant was brought to her place in the dock,
Then the jury filed in, eyes averted, from the accused in her little black frock.
Resembling a gathering of vultures the lawyers adjusted their gowns,
They were grim faced but sure that the verdict would soon send the guilty one down.
The air crackled hostile with hatred, for the evil deed she had done,
And they'd painted the face of Lucretia, while she stood in the dock deaf and dumb.
In judicial robes of scarlet the judge solemnly considered the scene,
He'd observed the defendant minutely, and his instincts were troubling him.
His impartiality was paramount. A judge must delve deep for the truth,

Explore all mitigation, and question the burden of proof.
The evidence from prosecuting counsel was unequivocal, a man was dead,
The accused had confessed she had killed him, but no further words had she said.
Now the expert was called, the oath taken, her case files flagged for the Defence,
Permission to quote from them granted, for her task that last day was immense.
In the gallery the reporters lurked smugly their headlines already planned out,
They wanted a verdict of `Guilty`, for every street vendor to shout.
In the court not one soul thought her innocent.. She had killed in a most brutal way,
But the case could not reach its conclusion,till they`d heard what the expert would say.
All eyes were now fixed on the witness, and the woman she`d come to defend,
The prosecutor smiled discreetly, and enquired what new light she could lend?

WITNESS
My client was referred by her doctor as he feared she might take her own life;
But the woman I met was in desperate need, and criminally abused as a wife.
Each meeting was fully recorded, and the court possess six of my tapes
They are entered as mitigating evidence, and harrowing listening they make.

NARRATOR
The prosecuting counsel objected, but the judge overruled the

complaint,
And instructed that the expert continue, which she did without further restraint.

WITNESS
My client was clearly in trauma, but my efforts to help her in vain,
The Police Service demurred from involvement, and Social Services did much the same.
The first time I met the defendant she was overwhelmed by tears.

DEFENDANT (AS RECORDED)
I'm in a dreadful dilemma, and I can't eat or sleep for my fears.

WITNESS
Very briefly she'd nodded a greeting, as I ushered her to a chair,
Then she seemed to lose her power of speech, so deep was her painful despair.
She crouched in her shroud of silence, for what seemed a very long while,
Then recovered herself, with an effort, and grimaced an anguished smile.

DEFENDANT (AS RECORDED)
I was young when I met my husband. He seemed kind-hearted, and jolly and bright,
But my friends warned me to be cautious; he was not what he seemed at first sight.
In anger I rejected their cautions, accusing them of jealousy and spite,
We quarreled and my dear friends departed. I'd no idea, that they would prove right.
My naivety was my undoing, but I trusted that man with my life,
Believed all his tales of betrayal, even though I was to be his

fourth wife.
He said all his wives had been witches, and as mad as lunatic hares,
They`d abused him and stolen his money, and I was the first girl who`d cared.
He was clever at plausible stories, as he reeled me in to his net;
Perhaps we believe what we want to, or I was the most stupid one yet.

WITNESS
I passed her a box of tissues without comment of any kind
And as I watched her nervous reactions, I could see she`d a troubled mind.
Her face wore a perplexing darkness and she smoldered behind a blank stare,
Trembling with a terrible secret, she seemed scarcely to know I was there.
Each week we met for one hour, but little more was said,
I knew she was enduring violence, and saw injuries to her head.
The dark glasses she wore served a purpose, like the bandage around her wrist,
While the purple bruises around her neck were not where she`d been kissed.
Sometimes, as the recordings will testify, she broke into uncontrolled tears,
But for many weeks she stayed silent, and I learned little more of her fears.
Until the last morning when I saw her, and her sad eyes looked straight into mine.

DEFENDANT (AS RECORDED)
For me there is no future, now I`ve reached the end-of-the-line.

WITNESS

'But You're doing fine,' I told her. 'Please trust me and say how you feel,
I haven't come here to judge you, for I know that your suffering is real.'
Suddenly an avalanche exploded, and her grief cascaded like snow
Churning her with hysterical weeping, she was prostrate, with nowhere to go.
I encouraged her to be calmer, and tried to slow the pace,
Then she collapsed like a worn-out runner, who is weary from a long race.

NARRATOR
The witness now turned to her papers, while the judge referenced bundles and files.

WITNESS
I propose to play the recordings, for the evidence was carefully compiled.
You will hear my client speaking, without any prompting of mine,
For her suffering lasted for ten long years, before the purported crime.

NARRATOR
There was shuffling and passing of documents, as the barristers ransacked their notes,
And the jury leaned forward intently, this new evidence might impact their votes.

DEFENDANT (AS RECORDED)
I came with love to my marriage, but he brought a heart of stone,
Soon behind closed doors, the abuse began, whenever we were alone.
To the eyes of the world he was generous, a bonhomme, a manly

bloke,
But he was a `Street-god, House-devil,` beating me his idea of a joke.
Within days I experienced this violence, and his screaming outbursts of rage;
All the warnings I'd ignored came to haunt me, for now I was trapped in a cage.
First he coerced my family inheritance, and claimed he now had legal right,
And I was so desperate for his affection, like a coward I put up no fight.
Once he'd had all my property transferred, on my money his greedy eyes turned,
`Where did my millions, lie hidden?` Then he started the cigarette burns …

WITNESS
Her voice was a tormented whisper, as though choked by an iron band,
I waited and glanced at her briefly, then reached over and patted her hand.
She was cold to my touch and unflinching, detached from my curious eyes,
By her flat and monotonous manner, I knew I was not listening to lies.
I have since checked Land Registry transfers, and the house was transferred to his name,
That man was a vindictive criminal and this marriage just one part of his game.

DEFENDANT (AS RECORDED)
Love's story for me was a short one that fled like a mist from my life,
I found myself married to Jekyll and Hyde,and not valued at all

as a wife.
How I've yearned for a life that is peaceful, and prayed for release from the strife;
But his violence grew as the years passed; many times I have feared for my life.
That volcano always was bubbling, I trod the hot coals of my fears.
If THIS is LOVE, what is HATRED? I've pondered that question for years.
He twisted my brain like a corkscrew, wiped mud from his shoes with my hair;
Battered me daily with insults, and tied me for hours to a chair.
He screams that I'm idle and useless, that I haven't the brains of a rat;
Says I'm not in his league, and surplus to need; that I'm old and I'm ugly and fat.
When his adrenalin surge begins rising, hatred's carved in each line of his face,
I shrivel inside when I look in his eyes, for I know there is no hiding place.
He has driven away those who loved me, turned my life into one living hell,
Pushed me right to the edge of madness, I've no family or friends left to tell.
All that I had he has taken from me, and abused me worse than a slave;
Warned me I will never escape him, until I lie dead in my grave.
He took my clothes and burnt them, and threw me into the street,
And forced me to plead on my hands and knees, when I needed food to eat.
With him I cannot argue; he decides what is right and what's wrong,
And he takes kitchen knives to gouge out my eyes, if I'm out of the house for too long.

He mocks me and says that I`m clumsy, always bumping and banging around,
But his pals at the pub think he`s generous and good, and I`m crazy and mentally unsound.
Last week he left me senseless when he threw me down the stairs,
But he laughed and said who`d believe me, no one likes me and no one cares.
How can I fight against him? He`s too plausible, crafty and strong.
Whatever he does against me, I will always appear in the wrong.
How I`ve yearned to escape into silence, in some place where no anger is heard,
Or go to sleep and never wake up, or just fly away like a bird.
My doctor advised me to leave him, not stay for one moment more.
But he found the place I was hiding, and beat me and called me a whore.
He bound my wrists and he gagged me, screaming I was out of my mind,
Then threw me into a cupboard and pad-locked the door behind.
He laughed to hear me choking and told me to get used to the smell
For I`d seen my last rays of sunshine and soon I`d be rotting in Hell.
I struggled all night in bleak darkness while I fought to break free from my plight,
And by daybreak I`d sprung the door open! I had to go on with the fight.
When you`re locked in a terrible conflict, and you fear that your enemy will win
The last battle must be for survival, and I knew now I couldn`t give in.

WITNESS

She opened her bag and I watched her, as she unwrapped a
blood-stained knife;

DEFENDANT (AS RECORDED)
This morning before I came here, I ended his god-damned life.
I watched him lying there snoring, then pushed this blade into his
head;
Ten years of his vicious hatred are finished. I've killed him. He's
DEAD.

WITNESS
Her words were bleak and hopeless and came from a broken
heart.
Then she raised the veil across her face and I saw she was torn
apart.
Her eyes were bruised and swollen, her neck and mouth chaffed
raw,
And her fingers and hands were bleeding from tearing at her
prison door.
She slumped to the floor in a stupor still clutching the gory knife,
And I prized it gently from her before she could end her life.

NARRATOR
As the witness's evidence concluded, the courtroom fell silent and
dazed,
For the poignancy of those recorded words left the opposing
counsels fazed.
For weeks the case had focused upon the woman's purported
crime,
And dumbly she'd made no effort to defend herself during that
time.
For years she'd been beaten and conditioned into silently
accepting blame,
And from the court she'd expected no mercy only bitter

castigation and shame.
The judge was not swayed by pity, but by revelations of terror and dread.
The new evidence was compelling, concerning the man who was dead.
For a moment he sagely reflected, before the public gallery erupted in noise,
And he was moved to turn his anger on restoring decorum and poise.
Once the ushers had cleared the courtroom, he solemnly resumed his place,
There was controlled rage in his bearing, and the power of the Law on his face.
The Jury was asked to retire while the case was adjourned overnight;
For he needed time to consider the malfeasance now come to light.
This case must be declared a `Mistrial` for no other verdict would stand,
There had been prejudicial malpractice, with the suppression of evidence planned.
In his chambers both legal teams gathered, where His Honour demanded to know.

JUDGE
Why was the defendant abandoned for ten months before this fiasco?
I'm appalled by such legal incompetence, and the vital facts never revealed;
Because she had signed a confession, did you judge that her fate had been sealed?
You prepared a brief of token evidence, while she languished in prison on remand,
Is this what you purport to be justice, and conjecture the Law of

Our Land?
Marriage is a legal institution where each partner holds equality of rights,
It is not a legalized bondage, where with impunity a man may abuse his wife.
All acts of violence are criminal, including coercion and verbal abuse,
Our laws regard all breeches as abhorrent, and marriage permits no excuse.
Defence Counsel has failed, abysmally, to reveal circumstances predating the crime,
And ignored mitigating, WHY, WHENS and WHEREFORES!
You had ten months of preparation time!
Without the evidence of the expert witness we would never have learned the truth,
Shamefully you disregarded that Rule of Justice, which relies heavily on the `Burden of Proof`.
In Law we value The Presumption Of Innocence, until guilt is unquestionably proved.
Justice must protect the defenceless, with lawful means accessed and used.
Ending a life is Murder, when deliberate malice predicates the crime,
And Murder is frequently committed, during felonious acts of innumerable kinds.
But the case which was brought here before me lies outside the range of such acts,
The defendant showed no premeditation, which I accept as a now proven fact.
You brought to trial a victim, abused and driven half out of her mind
By the violence of her psychotic husband, a disgrace to human kind.
We are lawyers, and must administer justice, this is no jungle

where `might is right`,
And the evidence speaks of her gentle nature. She was never provoked to a fight.
The story of her vicious degradation will be published in the Public Domain,
And as representatives of our system of Justice, I hope you sincerely feel shame.
I find no evidence of premeditation, in her torment she did not plan how to act;
Every living human being has a breaking point, and that morning, blind fear made her snap.
In these circumstances I do not see her as `Guilty`, for she has suffered gravely under duress and strife,
What was done came from mind-bending terror, in defence of her own threatened life.
My directions will be clear to the Jury, no retribution is demanded in Law,
She has languished for ten months in prison, and in mercy I will not seek more.
She will leave my court a free woman, with no blot or stain of crime,
And may God lay His Mercy upon her, and grant her peace in the fullness of time.

---ooOoo---

A performed recording of the above (and other pieces) may be obtained from any of the following:
www.audioarcadia.com
www.audible.com
www.audible.co.uk
www.audiobooks.com

SURFING OFF A BEACH OF DIAMONDS

Chris Holt

It came in on a neap tide. Kelso saw it first and sprinted into the sea. Michael Tregarth, his grandfarther, watched him swim out to a greenish orb bobbing up and down between the breakers. He cupped his hands and shouted to him:

'Leave it, Kelso. Leave it, lad.' But the old man's voice was lost in high wind and the wails of gulls.

A woman draped in a towel stopped and followed Tregarth's gaze. 'What's he after?'

'A pod from the Gulf Stream. He should let it go.'

'Why?'

The old man pointed. 'Look at the undertow. It's taking it out again. Neptune wants it back.'

'How weird.' She padded off through the sand.

Kelso emerged from the water clasping his prize and ran to his grandfather. 'What's this, Garth?'

Tregarth laughed. 'It's a *whole* coconut, not just the endocarp you get in a supermarket. Now put it back, Kelso.'

Kelso frowned. 'Put it back? I don't understand,' he said, yet he understood very well what his grandfather meant. 'But can I draw it first and return it tomorrow?'

'All right, tomorrow.'

'Thanks, Garth.'

Kelso had been calling his grandfather 'Garth' since he was three years old. Tregarth, who had once been a science teacher, had now retired to his coastal cottage, where he finally indulged his life-long interest in astronomy. But when the surf was up he would drag out his Bob Shepherd long board and turtle-roll out to the line of breakers. His choice made, his taut body would arch and with the soles of his feet firm on the waxed board he would ride the high surge, a brief sculpture of sinew and muscle on the tumbling horizon.

School holidays brought him Kelso, a boy who was never bored, especially at the sea. This was borne out by his art. Kelso had shown a rare talent from the time he first picked up a crayon. Now at twelve years old he had already won two Open Awards at the County Festival.

Back at the cottage, Kelso set the coconut up on the patio for a still life. Before sketching he scrutinised it for nearly a quarter of an hour. He decided that it looked more yellow than green, the colour of a half-ripe banana, with a smooth skin overlaying its dips and swellings.

'Just make sure it goes back tomorrow. It'll look happier then. And so will I.'

'You're just giving in to superstition, Garth.'

'*No!*' Tregarth's retort made Kelso flinch.'Don't you understand? That thing doesn't belong here. The ocean currents must carry it back to the tropics – to some coral atoll where it can germinate. Neptune knows best.'

'Neptune is a planet.'

'And the god of the sea! The two are related. There'll be a clear sky tonight, and I'll show you something.

At 2am Garth set up his telescope. He woke Kelso who pulled a roll-neck jumper over his pyjamas and followed his grandfather out onto the patio. There was no moon but the glow of far-off galaxies gave a warming backdrop to the more neighbourly bodies of the night sky. Mars glowed like new copper. Jupiter blazed.

Tregarth had connected the telescope to a lap-top. Silent minutes passed as he adjusted the focus. Then he stood back and turned to Kelso with a look of triumph and pointed to the lap-top.

'Neptune,' he said, 'centre screen.'

Kelso crouched down to observe a disc of light so tiny that

the boy had to squint to see it at all. But, when he did, it was a revelation. 'It's *blue. Gentian* blue, nearly purple. How can it be that colour?'

'The planet is mostly ocean, but not H2O; it's an ocean of methane and ammonia. That's where it gets its colour. I told you there was a connection with the sea.'

'Too cold for life, then.' Kelso straightened up.

'Yes, at least for hydro-carbon bodies like ours, but for others it could be rather fun.'

'How so, Garth?'

'Well, just think of it. Imagine surfing waves a hundred feet high and travelling at five hundred miles an hour. Wouldn't that be something?'

'In your dreams!'

'I don't think there's much wrong with dreams. Perhaps we need to become more open to possibilities.'

Kelso knelt down once more to see the blue planet. 'What else is on Neptune?'

'You want more? Well, consider this. During a storm it would rain diamonds … billions of them.'

'Diamonds?' This sounded fanciful to the point of absurdity; but Kelso had long made the distinction between his grandfather's bizarre beliefs and the old man's science.

'They'd be caused by the breakdown of methane. Beaches heaped high with crystalline carbon: pebble-sized diamonds. Now we'd best be getting back to sleep.'

Just before they went inside, Kelso noticed that there was something missing. The coconut was lying at the bottom of the steps. It must have rolled off the table. The boy's thoughts were interrupted by Tregarth's voice. 'Don't forget the tide will start to go out about 8.30. I expect the coconut to be going out with it. Make sure it does.'

By the time Kelso got up next morning the land breeze had veered to a sea wind and he smelt the salt air. In daylight the coconut looked almost innocuous. He wondered what lay under the smooth skin. If he could just cut out a sliver, not enough to do real damage. He'd just take enough to do a botanical study – a few pen lines and an ink wash. He carried the pod to his grandfather's shed.

He tried the first incision with a fishing knife but the operation was harder than he had imagined. Twice he nearly cut his hand. The thing was a husk of fibre. From somewhere he remembered the word *coir*. He abandoned the knife and took up a tenon saw. Reddish coir littered the ground before he eventually sawed into softer matter. Juice squirted into his eyes and he felt something come away.

In disgust he wiped his sleeve and looked down. There at his feet was a severed plant, its one exotic leaf drooping like a torn pennant. He recoiled from the pod which spun off the bench, bounced on the stone paving, and ejected the endocarp, which wheeled across the floor and came to rest by the wheelbarrow. The endocarp had a reddish 'monkey-face' with two flat 'eyes' and a 'mouth'. Kelso stared at what he had done and his heart pounded. Worse came when he heard his grandfather's voice at the shed door.

'You've killed it,' said Tregarth.

'I didn't mean to. I'll still put it back in the sea.'

'And dare mock the ocean with another outrage? Just leave it be. I'll clean it up later.

'Let me clean it up. I'm really sorry, Garth.'

'Leave it , I say, or worse might befall 'ee.'

Another boy might have laughed at his grandfather's reversion to archaism but Kelso caught the ancestral echo. A vengeful Neptune suddenly seemed as normal as a creaking branch. Despite Tregarth's wishes, as soon as he left, Kelso swept up the coir and dropped it into a hessian sack with the rest of the pod. He picked up the endocarp and shuddered. With its hairy feel it was more like a monkey's head than ever. He retched and almost dropped it.

The calm surface of the ocean was pocked like beaten metal. Kelso winced with the cold as the eddies splashed against his calves. He upturned the sack and felt relief as he saw the contents drifting out. He felt the ebb tide dragging at his ankles.

But as he turned to go back there was a gentle bump against his leg. A mischievous wavelet had flung back the endocarp. There was the monkey's head again, rotating in the swirls, its red fur hackling in the foam and its lifeless face playing a ghastly peekaboo.

Kelso dipped down, seized it with one hand and hurled it further out, praying that the current would take it from his life forever. At first he thought he had his wish for he saw it bobbing away, losing itself in the low troughs and rising with the crests. But then a swell rose like a monster under sheets, and lifted it right back onto the beach.

The boy groaned. He tore off his shirt and vest, dumped them both in a pile over his shoes, snatched up the endocarp and ran into the waves. Grasping it in one hand he struck out with an awkward side stroke into deeper water where he let it go.

It was then the surf awoke like an angry dog. The freed endocarp shot a foot into the air, to plop down by the boy's face.

'Go!' Kelso cried out. 'Just GO AWAY!'

And the thing obliged, or at least it obeyed the outgoing tide. But to his dismay Kelso found himself way out of his depth and drifting after it. He put his face below the surface to see the bottom but there was only a green vault. Vertigo seized him and he tried to calm himself.

'I mustn't panic. Must keep parallel to the shore!' He was drifting faster. There was a deadness. The shore gulls were inaudible. All he could hear was the slap of water against his body. He wasn't alone. Keeping pace with him and only six yards ahead was the hairy skull of the endocarp. Twenty minutes passed. The boy swallowed water with each breath. He felt sleepy.

'Kelso!' The cry was behind him still far off. 'Kelso!' Now stirred to full consciousness the boy turned his head to see Tregarth flat down and duck paddling towards him. His long board shearing the swells until he drew up alongside his grandson. He dragged the boy over the board, unhitched his own foot leash, clamped it around Kelso's ankle and turned to shore.

The boy mouthed the words 'thank you' and spewed out salt water. Tregarth slapped his shoulder. 'Hold on.' The escaping tide had quickened the undertow and the surfboard struggled in the cross currents. Tregaarth leant forward to keep the nose on point. But as they reached the first line of homing breakers, Neptune vented his spite. Without warning a claw of green water snatched the old man into the depths. The same wave lifted the board twelve feet into the air. Kelso cried out in raw fear as he was tunnelled into a second breaker which swept him to shore. The boy had barely unleashed his foot when the ebb flow dragged the board back to sea.

For a week rescue helicopters pursued forty sightings of major flotsam. Volunteers scoured the tidelines but Tregarth's body was never recovered,

Kelso went on to become a leading marine artist. His *Beloved Surfer* is in the Falmouth gallery. The painting has its critics. They complain that the sea is painted an unearthly purple, the surfer is minuscule when compared to the waves and the beach in the foreground is heaped with diamonds.

---ooOoo---

THE CHRISTMAS CLUB

Helen Hudgell

The village was hunkered down for the long, harsh winter; a dark, amorphous rats' nest where the huddled inhabitants scavenged for survival. The short hours of stark daylight were resented and endured, heightening, as they did, awareness of their inescapable, gnawing need. Nights were a welcome, if temporary, relief from relentless anxiety. When concealing darkness fell, few lights shone for long, as early bed saved money and sleep staved off hunger's bite. Even the smoke that trickled from the chimneys was thin. Children were sent out each day, armed with sacks and barrows to search the slag heaps for lumps of coal. But the pickings were limited. There were often scraps over the meagre finds. Fearful of returning empty-handed, they would continue burrowing through the detritus until the gloaming drove them home, wearily dragging their scanty spoil, knowing it would never be enough.

Money was tight and times were hard. They always were but this year was worse. The pitmen were on strike and the pit owners were determined to starve them back. This determination was fuelled by the power of money and, so certain were they of success, they had offered the men not a rise but a decrease in wages. Obdurate resentment was building on both sides. The villagers, of course, bore the brunt and, when the gentry drove past in their shiny, expensive cars with their well-fed, well-dressed families, if angry, scared men spat in the gutters, who could blame them? Equally, if there was some redistribution of wealth, when those who worked in the big houses came home on their days off with bags and baskets containing left-over food and scraps, who should be surprised?

For hunger was the bogeyman who stalked the streets and

peered in through the small windows, smirking when he heard the cries of underfed children. He liked it best when he heard women sobbing because he knew that another, small soul had given up the fight. And, a fight it was. The women knew it and their fear showed in their eyes; fear for their children and fear for their men. They battled deprivation with every weapon they could muster. Every penny was stretched to its limit. The relief they felt every time a meatless stew was consumed, or a stale loaf gobbled, was immediately replaced with the worry of where the next meal was coming from. They, of course, ate little, saying, "I've already had mine," or, "I'm not hungry." Excuses they tried to hide behind, as their faces grew gaunter and their clothes hung on them.

As the days grew shorter and the nights longer, fear increased. Christmas was coming and the children, despite the remorseless reality that surrounded them, were excited. The overriding aim became to give the children a good day. Fathers whittled simple dolls that mothers would dress in clothes fashioned from rags. Wooden trucks and dollies' cradles were constructed, painted and hidden in sheds. Unravelled jumpers were reknitted as gloves and hats. Children painted and cut paper chains and planned the hoops of holly and ivy they would make to hang in the houses. And, then there was the Christmas Club. Even the adults felt a warm glow at the thought of the good meal they would have when the club paid out the year's collection. There might even be a bit left over for a few extras: some sweeties, hair ribbons, a new penny each for the children.

The Christmas Club was a long-established institution, set up and run in the Clubhouse. Each man's weekly donation was recorded in "The Book" and a running total kept. This year the task had fallen to Tommy Yardley, for, as his fellow members attested, "He's a canny lad. Tha can trust Tommy Yardley." Every Saturday night he would sit at a corner table with a glass of beer; his pay for the job. One by one the pitmen would come in, with a few pence scraped together for a pint which they would nurse all evening, and hand over to Tommy their couple of bob or pence "Our Lass" had managed to hold onto for Christmas. Once the savings were safely tucked away, the rest of the evening was spent in doling out strike pay. Special cases were considered, discussed and extra, small allocations made. Proud men, providers, defeated by the greed of their masters, shuffled over and bowed by shame, pocketed the few coins. Silent comrades, with wordless understanding, looked away or patted a recipient's shoulder.

Armed with the fleeting security of a few bob in their pockets, the men turned to talk of the continuing strike and strengthened one another's resolve to fight on. There would be no scabs here. Finally, they made their way home, feeling like men again; fighters in control of their lives. The glow lasted all the way home, only to be dissipated when they handed over their pittances of strike pay and saw the quickly hidden disappointment in their wives' faces.

Two weeks before Christmas was when the Club money was to be handed out. By the time Saturday night at last came, the village was buzzing with excitement. Children were asking eagerly, "Can I have barley sticks? Can I have a tram? A dolly with closing eyes? Red ribbons? Can I? Can I?" The wives, worries shelved temporarily, were discussing with one another, "Will I buy a capon which will last a few days and make a broth or maybe a joint and a couple of rabbits?" "Perhaps I can get some decent tea?" "Or blow it all on a bottle of gin!" one laughingly joked. "The old chap needs a new pair of boots. Do you think there will be enough for some? Second-hand would do."

The excitement was palpable as the men, for once with a spring their steps, left the houses to collect their hard saved money. The Club's yellow lights shone warmly in welcome as they approached. As the first few entered, they turned to the corner and looked for Tommy Yardley but his table was empty. This was surprising but not alarming, so they bought their beer and chatted animatedly, while they waited. Each time the door opened they looked up but it was never Tommy. As the Club quickly filled, disquiet spread.

"Has anybody seen Tommy?" "Has anybody heard anything?" Eventually, the disquiet turned to anger and apprehension. "Where is he? He knows we're waiting." "Someone needs to go and get him."

"All right, lads. All right," said the Club Secretary. "Let's calm down. George and I will gan down and see what's keeping him."

Somewhat pacified the men continued talking, speculating. At long last, the door opened and with a blast of icy air, the two messengers entered. Silence. All eyes fixed. "He's gan." Silence. "The money's gan." Silence. Then uproar. "He's gan?" "Gan where?" "What does tha mean?"

"Listen! Listen! Tommy's gan. His lass disna kna where. She's in bits. It seems he used the money – for food and suchlike – thinking he could put it back. There's only a couple of pounds left. She disna kna where he is."

Emotions ran high: anger, followed by disbelief and, finally, by despair. Futile threats were hurled, filling the room. But they knew, in the end, they would have to go home and tell their waiting, expectant wives. The night became that much darker, the air that much colder.

In the days that followed a dull resignation set in. Mrs. Yardley and her children, unable to face the recriminations of their neighbours, did a flit. Neighbouring pits, hearing of the situation, had whip rounds and sent small amounts to be shared. Christmas came and went and, somehow, with the fortitude of the poor and the loving determination of parents, they made the best of it. The children had their gifts and, as with the miracle of the loaves and fishes, everyone had a meal on Christmas Day.

Nothing more was heard of Tommy Yardley, until, one day, early in the New Year, some children were in the woods gathering sticks. As they came charging into a clearing, carrion crows flew upwards, flapping, cawing. Before them was the swinging body of the missing man. They stood fascinated, gazing at the corpse, their eyes glued to the bird-ravaged, purple face. His long shadow circled the clearing, passing over their upturned faces, mesmerising them, burning his image into their brains. Eventually, one of the bolder boys ran over and pushed the hanging legs. As he swayed silently backwards and forwards, the children dispersed, screaming.

Later, some men came and cut him down. He was buried, without ceremony, in a pauper's grave with no stone to mark the place.

You might think that people would have felt sympathy for a man who was so trapped by his desperation that he saw no way out but to kill himself, but they didn't. They hated him for betraying them. For breaking the bonds that bound them. For exposing their vulnerability. It wasn't until years later that time, distance and better conditions enabled them to understand his actions, but never to forgive.

---ooOoo---

FOUR POEMS

Briony Kapoor

1. Strange Intimate Union

Earth is the body of the disembodied pure
Here we are grounded our ideals are sure
Rendered of deep dark seeming is more rare
But by a passion all of us are found
To be of earth and yet ourselves earthbound
Nor alone the earth, nor by itself the air
As in their union strange intimate the pure

Who taught me that desire is cosmic
To my such yearning I should yield myself
Throw round my arms grand to embrace this earth
With grave exultance in the beauty absolute
Of dark love bound to sing about its form
Time swelled heart in ages contemplate
Being more mighty than a thousand worlds
While sweated brow with diamond drops and pearls
Scatter about enormous strides to take
And learn at last slow beauty of the work?

This is a poem acknowledging the possibility or indeed the reality of God in everything. It distinguishes between the material and the sublime but recognises our participation in both and concludes that envisioning the one within the other is the best approach. It combines the idea of the glory of God from the Christian tradition with the universality of God in the Hindu one.

2. Who Live Upon a Mountain

Are we in the world
Who live upon a mountain?
So many layers in the sky
And levels solid passing up to grey
Am I the bright light
Pouring in through there
Or am I moistured green
Like leaves dissolved in air?
How may a valiant daisy
Dare to face this life
Throw challenge to an oak tree
I, too, am here on earth?

Some of the rain that's falling
Lies here upon the lawn
While some deep to the valley
Will down and down be drawn
That which above, my soul,
The sunlight clearly lit
Below do mingle, alas,
In the mud and grit

This poem sees the divine within the natural again comparing the highest possible states attainable with the lower ones of which we are capable. It recognises the possibility of perfection (God) and the marvel of creation in all things no matter what their apparent form.

Both these poems (1 & 2) were written in the Himalayas the second one during the monsoon when the weather patterns, the light and the landscape are dramatic.

3. Darling I cannot …

Darling I cannot meet your eyes
I love your modest, moral
And your steadfast ways
My eyes would, guileless,
Tell you everything
Desire for me would
Revolution
To your manner bring
Sweetly contained, thus,
Near your person, I
Softly radiant, inward know
Which could not from
Lovemaking eyes
Towards you, outward, flow

This one, a love poem, is self explanatory I think.

4. Mosquito

Mosquito tumbling
Sideways in the air
Tickling my arm and
Tangling in my hair
I hear your singing hum
And know you're there.
Why should I dread your
Presence and your sting
If we are both
Created from one thing?
If feasting on my blood
Your satisfaction is
Then drink your fill
While I lie here in peace.
My God expanded heart
My fretted nerves will ease
And you, my little darling,
May do just as you please.

This cheerful little poem at a deeper level puts faith to the test in an everyday event. Or it might be seen as something of an exercise in meditation.

---ooOoo---

AT THE BOTTOM OF THE STAIRS

Kate Lockwood Jefford

I was eight years old and standing at the bottom of the stairs at my grandparents' house when the 'phone rang on what became the day that, forever after, my mother measured all time against. The 'phone was heavy and black, Bakelite, the sort people pay big money for at vintage fairs these days. It sat in the hallway on its own table with a shelf underneath for the thick, arm-aching directories of the time. From this vantage point it observed all comings and goings, that morning I and my three sisters racing around the circuit we'd formed by opening all interconnecting doors between hall, kitchen, and lounge. After our pokey flat the other side of the city, we revelled in the enormity of a proper house with stairs to slide down or jump from. We made it our playground every time we came to stay, which was often.

That summer morning we ignored the gentle chastisement of our grandparents, "Girls, let your breakfast go down. You'll get a stitch!" and shrieked with excitement. Our father was due back that afternoon, having been working away for the past fortnight, and we anticipated the rough and tumble games he played with us.

My mother would shout, "Paul, stop that, you'll hurt them!" He'd wink at us and pretend to be sorry, "All right, love, just after I've done this!" Then he'd whoop one of us up (not Mil who was nervous and stiff) and spin us like a disc above his head as we screamed with delight.

We weren't allowed to answer the 'phone, which was Nana's prerogative; she'd bustle towards it, wiping her kitchen hands on her pinny and patting her hair as if she were, in fact, answering the door.

However, that morning she had her hands in the sink so it was Grandfather who strode towards it, almost tripping over knee-high Lottie, and picked up the receiver.

"66804. Hello?"

I paused, curious, causing a pile-up of squealing siblings behind me.

It wasn't late at night, when the 'phone ringing triggered the adults to look at the clock with grave expressions and mutter, "Who on earth could be calling at this hour?" So I wasn't expecting Grandfather's frown that made his eyebrows bulge as he covered the mouthpiece, waved a finger at us to hush, and called, "Aud, it's the Royal Infirmary, they want to speak to you."

I watched as my mother appeared and bobbed down the stairs in a pencil skirt, breasts bouncing beneath her polka-dot blouse, fiddling with her hair, employing Kirby grips to pin it into a French pleat. She knew how to put together a look that turned heads, despite humble means.

As she leaned over my head to take the 'phone from Grandfather, her plucked brows quivered and she bit on her lipstick-free morning lips, "Yes? Yes, I'm Mrs Jones."

I don't know what the voice from the Royal Infirmary said to my mother in the pause that followed, but I saw the effect, as if an invisible marksman shot a single, silent bullet into her heart. She dropped to the floor, soundlessly but for the clatter of the receiver onto the tiled floor, chipping the Bakelite.

Nana ran from the kitchen, gathered my mother into her soap-sudded arms and flashed a look of alarm at Grandfather who'd retrieved the phone and was speaking in hushed tones into it. Nana, jerking her head towards the back door, said to me, "Take them outside and play, will you? There's a good girl."

We gathered around the swing erected in our honour by Grandfather. I sat on the wooden seat with Lottie on my lap, swaying to-and-fro. Biddy hung upside down above our heads, knees and fists clasping the cross-bar, being a bat. Mil stood still nearby, mesmerised by a bee doing its rounds of the roses. I followed its path as it flew off toward the eaves of the house high above us, and caught a glimpse of Nana through an upstairs window, carrying my mother, limp as a rag-doll, head lolling on her chest.

My mother and Nana stayed upstairs for ages and Grandfather made our dinner at midday. The chips were burnt, but I covered mine in tomato sauce and ate them, and my sisters copied. Afterwards, we were taken into the living room and Nana and Grandfather stood in front of us, looking stern. We'd been good so it I knew they weren't going to tell us off.

Grandfather cleared his throat, "Your Daddy's had an accident. He won't be, um, coming home. Mummy's very sad. So be good girls, won't you?"

His voice sounded funny and if I didn't know better I'd have thought he was trying not to cry. Afterwards we sat on the front steps and Biddy shouted to all passers-by, "Daddy's had an accident and Mummy's in bed!"

Nobody told us when our father was coming back, or where he was. We had to figure that out for ourselves because the grown-ups were acting all funny, peculiar, not ha-ha. The little ones thought he was working to buy more presents for Christmas. In my eight-year-old mind, I figured he'd gone on his own holiday because he was fed up with us. I decided to be bright and funny so when he came back he wouldn't be disappointed and go away again. After a few days we went home and all my father's things were gone, confirming my belief that he'd packed up and left us to go on holiday by himself. Other kids at school didn't have fathers around. Annie Donovan's went away for five years before he came back. Julian Evans had never even met his.

I got into a fight in the playground with a girl who said my father was dead and I'd be waiting till I was a skeleton for him to come back. I pulled a handful of her hair out. I can still see the clump of ginger strands in my sweaty palm. We were sent to the headmistress who wore glasses on a gold chain round her neck, didn't look straight at us, and told us to say three Hail Marys.

Meanwhile, I carried on with the business of being good: making beds, running errands, doing the dishes, pegging out the washing, sweeping down the stairs. I looked after my sisters. My mother had become moody and irritable and took to her bed frequently. One rainy Saturday morning when I was about ten I took her a cup of tea. Since my father left, Saturdays were especially difficult for her and I hoped to cheer her up. I put the tea on her bedside table and opened the curtains.

"Hello, Mummy," I said.

She blinked in the light and said, "I've got a terrible headache, I think I'll stay in bed. Can you go to the shops for me? And pay the milkman when he calls, my purse is in the kitchen drawer."

My heart sank and I left her in the double-bed that dwarfed her without my father in his half. I marshalled my sisters into the bathroom to wash them and then helped them get dressed.

As we crept past the closed door of my mother's bedroom, Mil said, "Where's Mummy?"

"Mummy's too lazy to get up!" I said.
Before I knew what hit me, the door flew open and my mother, clutching her bri-nylon nightie tightly to her chest with her left hand, delivered a slap to the back of my head with her right, so hard it sent me reeling into the wall outside the bathroom where pen-marks recorded our annual growth.

"Oh, I am, am I?" she said. "I'll wash your mouth out with soap, young lady!"

She retreated, closing the door as I, flushed with shame, bit my tongue and blinked back burning tears.

Biddy took my hand and whispered, "Let's have a biscuit."

Mil patted my back and little Lottie clutched my leg. I remember experiencing a rush of gratitude for their love. That afternoon I took them to see "The Railway Children" at the Plaza. We all cried buckets and Lottie had a nose bleed all down her yellow dress.

It wasn't until halfway through my thirteenth year that I discovered my father wasn't coming back. I was revising for exams in the city library. I loved the library, the smell of polished parquet floors, the rows of books categorised on their shelves, the librarians atop their mobile stepladders. On a break from algebra, for which I had an inexplicable and somewhat useless gift, I was leafing through the national newspaper archives in the reading room. I wanted to be a journalist and this was one of my favourite things to do.

A headline in The Evening Herald of June 20th 1968 caught my eye and set my heart thumping so loud I thought the librarian would shush me.

"TRAGIC FATHER OF FOUR KILLED IN MIDSUMMER TRAIN CRASH."

The piece, two whole columns, gave my father's name and age, my mother's name and age, my name, my sisters' names and our ages. I read that he was keen to join his family and when his flight was cancelled due to a storm he caught the train instead. I must've cried out or something because a kind-faced lady librarian came over and asked me, quietly of course, if I was alright.

"Yes," I whispered, then prattled on, "it's just that my father's dead and I didn't know because I was only little and I thought he'd just gone away and, and-" I stood up, stumbled on jelly legs and then the sobs came, shuddering through me with such force I thought the top of my head would blow off.

The librarian pulled me to her and held me tightly, as if to stop me falling apart. She smelled of cigarettes and face-cream, and her woollen jumper was rough and reassuring on my damp skin.

I decided, from then on, that I wasn't going to be a good girl anymore. For the next five years I stormed through the rest of my adolescence, fighting tooth and nail with my mother.

I put up posters of pop-stars with sneering faces and she ripped them down so I put them up again. I stayed out late at weekends, drank American beer and smoked French cigarettes. I rolled up the waistband of my school uniform to show more leg. I got a Saturday job and spent my wages on lipstick and mascara. I went on the pill. I lost my virginity at fifteen against the back wall of a pub with a University student in a leather jacket who thought I was twenty. I couldn't sit down on the school bus the next day and it put me off sex for ages but I'd "done it" at last, earning the respect of my peers.

My mother didn't know what to do with me. Our rows caused my sisters to cry and the neighbours to bang on the walls. I went to live with Nana and Grandfather. That meant three buses to school and missing my sisters, but I had to get away from her. In the summer of my eighteenth year she took my sisters to Spain, the first holiday they'd had since my father died.

The day they were due back Nana and Grandfather drove to the airport to pick them up and I stayed back at the house, not yet ready to face my mother. So it was me who answered the 'phone at the bottom of the stairs when she rang to find out why they hadn't turned up.

---ooOoo---

JUST ANOTHER DAY

Martin Posnett

Heather Wilson, doctor in charge of A&E, was nearing the end of a 12-hour shift. Her holidays were only eleven days away. She was tired and the break would be most welcome. Ten days on a Greek Island, nothing to do except read books, lie in the sun, eat good food, and drink.

"Well what do you think?"

A small group of red spots grouped in a circle just under a right arm is under inspection.

"Flea bites?" The first-week junior doctor suggests from under the arm.

"Maybe…but no; its shingles, the beginning of a painful few weeks for you I'm afraid. It's probably brought on by the stress of your first week here! Take this to the Pharmacy and then…[she puts on a stern voice] I don't want to see you here for the next two weeks OK. Come back then and we'll have another look. Now go. We'll cope without you…somehow"

She smiles and hands the prescription to the junior who is shaking her head.

"Look. Forget it. I had it myself, about four years ago, just after I took over here, actually. You'll be OK. Don't you worry about anything. You're doing fine. Just go home. Take the tablets, and rest." She hands the junior her white coat. The junior pulls her clothes into shape, puts the white coat back on, drapes her stethoscope around her neck and cuts a forlorn figure as she shuffles slowly out of the Casualty Department.

Heather remembers her own first day as an eager, bright eyed and passionate know-it-all junior doctor, thrust onto the ward, totally unprepared for the reality of it. Her nerve weakened, then collapsed, when faced with having to deal with real vomit and real blood from real people. Quickly she was avoiding responsibility, leaving people behind curtains, queues growing, injections waiting to happen.

She had no words of explanation prepared when the head of A&E found her hiding in the cloakroom. Where she had hoped for sympathy she received incomprehension that she had made it through medical school. Where she had hoped for a kind word, she found herself on a suspension and then, if she wanted to become the only thing she had ever dreamed of being, she had a fight to try and convince the authorities that she was worthy of keeping her place.

She would admit later that it had made her. She had vowed to make it clear to every eager, bright eyed, passionate, and unsuspecting junior doctor who stepped into her path since that, "the quicker you get it, the better."

Sound Bite Surgeons: "You make a wrong decision at the end of your shift because you're tired…it's still a wrong call. You make a wrong decision at the beginning of your shift when you're wide awake…it's still a wrong call."

Dead Pan Doctors: "You're having a bad day because you had a row you're your partner…well go and tell that to the parents with the eight year old son who you diagnosed with measles, who then comes back in an all singing all dancing ambulance full of Meningitis"

Heather watches her latest apprentice leave, picking her time before she calls out to her "Don't worry. You're doing well. Your job's safe. Get well, and when you come back we will catch up"

The junior turns smiles, shrugs her shoulders and waves as she pushes through the swing doors.

Heather wonders how long it would be before the junior becomes as frustrated with the pressures and restrictions placed on them as the rest of the Doctors within the hospital.

Bed Pan Doctors: "Always wash your hands…because they will wash theirs of you if you mess up" So many of her colleagues had moved into the private sector, justifying their move with the words "More chances more stethoscope for more freedom."

Maybe one day, I'll do the same (she thinks to herself as she walks through the ward).

Heretic Healers: "It's all about deflecting the infecting".

The clock says two hours left, but at least it's quiet, the only nightmares are for the individuals in the waiting room, nothing to cause the department concern. The skin under her left arm feels tender. Postherpetic Neuralgia, when you've had Shingles the nerves are prone to react to the first sign of stress. She pulls a screen around an empty bed, and sighs as she sits down, I'm tired but I'm not stressed (she says to herself). She lies back on the bed, her hand covering her eyes. She feels her body become heavy. She yawns. She sits up, checks her watch, they'll find me if they need me and she settles back again onto the bed. "Sleep when you can, it could all go wrong in the next minute"

The sound of an ambulance all-singing-all-dancing pulls her back from the edge of sleep. She can hear the wail as it reaches the roundabout at the end of the road, if it's serious someone will be shouting for me any second. She feels her body starting to tense in preparation. Relax for as long as you can, just one more minute, breathe deep, control your breathing…slower…slower. She hears the doors crash open; she recognizes the ambulance men's voices. They might not need me, wait…wait. As her pager vibrates the shout comes…

"Doctor Wilson! Doctor Wilson!"

She sits up swings off the bed, and walks quickly into the ward, nothing much surprised her any more, so her control was complete.

"RTA male, hit by a car, severe head and spinal injury, multiple fractures of both legs and right arm, lost a lot of blood, blood pressure falling"

"Straight into the OT please "

The nurse's actions slip into automatic, taking over from the Paramedics, transferring the trauma equipment. She goes into the wash area, the nurses are getting into green surgical gowns, one of them holds a gown for her, she slips her arms through and the nurse fastens up behind her. She washes her hands and forearms and pulls the surgical gloves into place. She backs through the swing doors into the surgical emergency room. The overhead lights are warm and bright, illuminating the patient. The team is cutting off the clothes, wiping as much blood from him as they can, preparing him for the initial exploratory surgery. She talks to the anaesthetist. You have to be careful with a head wound. They both know, but it makes sense to be clear, all playing the same game with the same cards.

The casualty's clothes are thrown into a corner as they are removed. A brown scuffed and crushed leather briefcase is already there, the clothes cover it as they land. She watches and in the final moments before she takes over, something far to the back of her mind shifts forward. She looks to the patient, head supported, the side of his face covered with a bloodied swab. Recognition shifts, something is in a place where it shouldn't be, she looks to the pile of clothes in the corner.

That shirt was hand-made (she notices).She walks to the head of the patient. That briefcase was a birthday present. She looks down onto a battered, bloodied, disfigured face she knows so well. Alex? Her mind…slips away from its moorings, beginning to spin, creating its own eddy, faster and faster. She could see him lying there, in front of her…but it didn't make sense Alex…this is my husband. Why are you here? The blood seeping through the swab, onto the table, stillness thick, growing around her. Her mind trapped in the draw of a cascading waterfall of thoughts grasps for security and fails to find a hold.

"ALEX!!!!!"

She placed no blame on the surgeons who took over from her, but had been unable to save his life. They had put him on a life support machine. Heather had been taken into the private room at the end of the ward. She had been there many times, talking to the relatives and friends of her own patients, trying to find a way of sharing the news. The Doctor, her colleague, Consultant Gareth Morgan, tried as well as he could but even his vast pool of aloof experience was tested by compassion as he spoke.

"Heather…you understand…there is…nothing we can do for Alex…it…it just gives you time to say…It just gives you time… that's all"

She made the right noises, the noises she had heard everyone else making. She noticed the pictures on the walls for the first time. Sunrise and sunset on opposite walls, sunflowers in the centre. She wondered would he go straight back to work? Alex had no family alive, no brothers or sisters. She had no one to ring, no one else to share this with. She approached her responses professionally. Her emotions began to mirror the sterile atmosphere she was used to and surrounded with. She tried to think clear thoughts, about their life together, to remember good times, but nothing made its way through. She tried to feel guilty about not feeling anything.

She spent the night of the accident on a chair next to his body. She didn't sleep she just watched him, watched for signs of life. His face was covered in bandages, his body hidden under a metal frame covered in sterile green sheets. Tubes snaking out from under them, attached to life supporting machines.

She watched him. There was nothing, just the click of the respirator as it forced the lungs. The monitor showed the monotonous, mechanical, leap of a regulated lifeless heart.
It's a body supporting machine that's all…there is no life here (she conclude)

She sat all night.

As the sun began to colour the sky, and as for the rest of the world, life begins again on just another day… she turned the support machine off.

It was not as hard as she thought or hoped it would be.

---ooOoo---

THE ORCHESTRA OF ATTENTION

Peter Sharpe

"Some are born great, some achieve greatness and some hire public relations officers" - Daniel J Boorstin

"In the next few minutes Mr Sturgeon, I will teach you all there is to know about persuasion."

Johnny Monaco (not his real name) clapped his hands once and then threw them out wide, like a preacher embracing his flock. He stared down from the first floor balcony at the masses below him. Mr Sturgeon, standing next to him, looked decidedly less impressed.

"Mr Monaco" Sturgeon addressed him. "I appreciate your enthusiasm but I am a businessman and my business is in trouble. Exocorp is eating into our share each and every day, we are on the edge. We are spending a lot of money on you and your services, what matters to me are results and when I'm going to get them."

Monaco smiled and turned to face Sturgeon, unfazed by this demand.

"Results? Yes, results. I believe it was Winston Churchill who once said that however beautiful the strategy, you should occasionally look at the results". Now, I am not one to deny our greatest leader his eloquent accuracy, but in this case, he was wrong. My results, your results, our results (appealing for empathy) are a consequence of my strategy. Please, indulge me for a few moments"

Sturgeon went to speak. Before he could get his words out, Monaco cut in.

"You see Mr Sturgeon, the building we are standing in is certainly an architectural wonder and is known by many names,

"The Cathedral of the Railways" for example. However, to most of us, it is just St Pancras Station. It is a place to depart and to arrive and for the hundreds below us, that is all they care about.

They have no idea we are here, observing their every move from this balcony. They are more concerned with rushing to the platform for the something past something train to Derby, with waiting for their loved ones to emerge from behind the ticket gates, with hoping that their mistress will be waiting for them when they get off the Eurostar in Paris. Frankly Mr Sturgeon, it doesn't matter what they are up to and nor do I care. The point is that each one of these people is an opportunity, an opportunity for us to send them a message, a message that inspires them to put their hands in their pockets and spend their money with your company.

You see Mr Sturgeon, I am not your ordinary PR man, in fact, I abhor the term, I am much more than that. A PR company may know where to put your message and where to maximise exposure but exposure is useless without action, and that is why I am here. I am a conductor and these people are my orchestra, I bring order out of chaos and consequently, orders to your company."

"So what exactly are you going to do Mr Monaco? How are you going to get these hundreds of people below us to do what we want?"

"Humans have spent thousands of years trying to get others to think a certain way. Most of the time, this was done with sheer physical force and intimidation, you will think the way I want to, or you will face the wrath of God! Well, I have no time nor inclination for such savagery. Why don't we just cut out the middle man and make people think something without them even knowing it? Isn't that the more elegant solution Mr Sturgeon?"

Sturgeon was still unimpressed

"Let us begin" Monaco proclaimed.

"Of the hundreds of people below us, three of them will soon make themselves known to us. Ah ha, there is number one, right on time!"

Monaco pointed to a woman, young, smartly dressed, attractive, emerging from the platforms on the east of the concourse. She made her way down the centre of the station, weaving in and out of the crowds, drawing stares from several of the other passengers. She stopped short of the news stand and produced a ringing phone from her designer handbag.

"That's a seven hundred pound phone, in a three thousand pound handbag, just waiting for someone to take it" Monaco said. "Player one is in place" He looked to the doors to the west of the station, about 50 yards from where the woman was standing. "And here, is player number two!"

Monaco pointed to a man making his way onto the concourse. He too was young, but less well presented. He walked with an awkward shuffle, but not without intention. He stopped and hovered near the escalators, 10 yards from the woman, eyeing her with a nervous stare.

"Now what?" Sturgeon enquired

"Now, Mr Sturgeon, the trap is set" Monaco pointed at the large clock overlooking the concourse. "The clock reads 7.29pm Mr Sturgeon, we have about 30 seconds"

The clock edged towards 7.30, the large, ornate hands moved into place. With the final movement, the young man took off from behind the elevators, moving quickly towards the woman. He manoeuvred himself behind her. In one motion, he snatched the phone from her ear and pushed her to the ground, hooking her falling bag onto his arm. He started running, quickly, back towards the entrance to the west.

"Perfect!" Monaco said to himself

It took one, maybe two seconds for the woman to comprehend what had happened, shaken out of her comfort zone, she began to scream. The mugger was at least 10 metres away by now, weaving through the crowds.

"What the hell are you doing!" Sturgeon demanded

"Attention management" Monaco said, matter-of-factly. "The

crowds have woken up Mr Sturgeon, all eyes are now on the figure heading towards the door. And, as they are the general public, they have no idea how to react to this situation, apart from stand and watch"

The mugger bobbed and weaved, pushing a young couple out of the way and onto the floor. No one dared come near him, some shouted, some shook their heads but his path to the door was clear. He was just 10 metres from disappearing off into the safety of Euston Road, where he could blend in with the crowds in the London evening.

Five metres, he sidestepped a young couple pushing a pram. Three metres, he lined himself up with exit, Two metres, he increased his pace slightly, One metre. Bang!

"Yes!" Monaco celebrated, spinning on the spot and clapping his hands.

The mugger fell to the floor hard, landing on his back awkwardly. The contents of the bag spilled out on the floor around him, the phone skidded a few metres away from him, coming to rest just in front of the couple with the pram.

"And there Mr Sturgeon is player number three. Take a look, do you recognise him?"

Sturgeon strained, looking at the man who had tackled the mugger. He was tall, at least six foot two, dressed in a business suit and camel overcoat, carrying a leather briefcase.

Sturgeon stuttered in disbelief. "That's, that's George Thomas, my Chief Executive." Thomas wrestled the mugger on the ground, forcing his hands behind his back and driving his knee into the base of his spine. The mugger yelped in pain, struggling to get free. A crowd of passengers had now gathered around the two. Some of them scrambled to produce their smartphones, photographing and videoing the scene.

The victim ran over, still shaken, and hurried to collect her belongings off the floor. Thomas looked up to acknowledge her and she smiled at him through her tears. He forced the mugger further into the ground. Two British Transport Police officers emerged from the crowd, hauling the mugger up and putting him in handcuffs.

Thomas stood back from the scene and fixed his tie. The crowd continued to film him with their phones, some started to applaud.

Up in the balcony, Monaco turned to Sturgeon. "You see Mr Sturgeon, pictures of Thomas will be all over the social networks tonight and thanks to my well placed contacts in the press, all over the news tomorrow. I can see the headlines now. Your company will have never been so popular, customers will beat a path to your door, all because of a simple act of public spirit." Monaco pulled out his phone. "Ah ha!" he proclaimed "the pictures are already trending online" He gleefully showed Sturgeon the screen.

Sturgeon turned away. "I can't believe you! You staged a mugging, here, in one of the busiest parts of London, what about the poor girl that was robbed? I can't accept this!"

"Relax Mr Sturgeon, they were all in on it from the start. Natalie works for me, nice girl and a brilliant actress. Likewise, the mugger works for me too. Nothing will happen to him, he might get a night in the cells but she will drop the charges in the morning, besides, he won't mind when he sees his payslip at the end of the month."

"And George?" Sturgeon asked.

"Yep" Monaco replied, he was in on it as well. I have been in discussion with him for weeks, we even got an expert in to teach him those restraining moves." Monaco faced Sturgeon. "No one was hurt, no harm has been done, your company is saved and we all win. Not bad for a few minutes work eh?" he grinned. "The perfect publicity stunt"

Sturgeon looked down from the balcony, turned and walked away towards the escalator. "We will see in the morning Mr Monaco, we will see." And with that he walked away into the busy London night.

Monaco let out a sigh and looked down at the crowds of people below him. Normal life had resumed. "Well done my orchestra" he thought to himself "you played well, but tomorrow is another day and we have a new score to learn. Never forget that every moment is a chance to change someone's mind."

Postscript

Dear reader,

    I am interested in how you feel about Mr Monaco. Hopefully, you will see him as a liar. Someone who will shamelessly mislead and deceive for nothing more than commercial gain. If so, then this story has worked just as I wanted it to. Mr Monaco does exist and he is, in fact, my biggest rival in the PR world. However, that's where the truth stops. "The Truth", in this case is slightly more interesting. Monaco wasn't at St Pancras, none of the people in this story were. It is a complete work of fiction. But, I hope it planted an idea in your head about who he might be and as a consequence, you will never give him or any of his clients the time of day.

    As he said, every moment is a chance to change someone's mind. If I have changed yours, to the negative, then my work is done and you are as much a part of this story as any of the other characters. Always question what's in front of you, take nothing at face value.

    Regards,

Your unreliable narrator. Public Relations Officer, Exocorp

---ooOoo---

FERDIE

Michele Sheldon

He'd told all her friends that they'd met at the disco diva night. She'd gone as Agnetha from Abba and worn a long blonde wig, a bright blue satin cat suit and a pair of 4ins platform boots that made her feel like she ruled the world, until the cider kicked in. Their eyes had met over two drunk Bee Gee-lookalikes rolling around the floor. *It was love at first sight and we danced all night*, he'd say in his languid Brazilian accent. And then he'd come back to her flat and never left. He'd told the story so many times that she'd begun to believe it. But recently a niggling little voice had started sneaking up on her between sleep and consciousness when it would yell: *It's not true. None of it's true.* And it would send her heart racing and her head reeling because she knew exactly who he was. She'd tried to tell her sister. But she'd just laughed. You're *off your rocker. You're demented.* And now the truth had become one big, fat joke.

'But don't you think it's too much of a coincidence?' said Alex.
'Oh, not this old chestnut again,' replied her sister down the phone.
'Well, don't you?'
'No, for the millionth time he's just moved on to some other mug's house. Cats are like Royalty. They have homes all over the place.'
'You've never liked him...ever since he bit you.'
'Don't be ridiculous.'
'I'm not...but it doesn't feel right.'
'Hello! That'll be reality kicking in...'

'No, no, it's not that. He's just so nice and kind and considerate. All the time. It's not normal,' she whispered just as Ferdie walked into the room with her dinner. He placed it on the table and mouthed: 'Come and eat before it goes cold,' before disappearing into the kitchen.

Alex peered at the plate and her appetite died.

'Oh, God. It's fish again; grilled salmon. Tuna yesterday. Mackerel the day before. I'm sick of it,' whispered Alex, unlocking the French doors.

'Oh, please. You're so ungrateful.'

'I *am* not,' said Alex, taking the phone away from her ear to slide the doors open. She stepped out onto the patio and put the phone back to her ear just in time to hear Ella saying:

'.. always complaining about him. But you've got nothing to complain about.'

'But I...I...' Alex said, trying to interrupt as she walked to the end of garden.

'No, you listen to me. I wish I had someone like Ferdie to look after me. But I'm on my own. I have to do ev-er-y-THING.'

'But it's not right,' Alex said, glancing behind her, checking Ferdie wasn't in earshot 'He's not who you think he is.'

'For God's sake, Alex. Just STOP IT.'

Alex momentarily held the phone away from her ear, her sister's voice tinny and distant.

'I've got to go. I'm late making tea for the kids. I don't have a Ferdie to look after me. Bye-bye!'

Alex quickly placed the phone to her ear.

'No! Please...I think he's seeing someone else. Ella? Ella?' she whispered. But the line was dead. She stuffed the phone into her pocket, suddenly aware of being watched. She looked up. Two slits of orange in a huge mass of long grey fur stared down at her from the garden wall; Princess Tara, her neighbour's new cat. 'You eavesdropping hairy-arsed freak,' Alex spat as she clapped her hands. 'Go away!'

In return, Princess Tara arched her back and hissed. Alex stepped back at the sight of her fangs. They reminded her of a cobra's teeth. And she wouldn't have been surprised if they contained venom.

Alex bent down and scooped up several pebbles from a pot plant and threw them at the wall. The cat gave a final hiss before disappearing.

'Oh, was that the Princess I just saw?' called Ferdie, poking his head through the patio doors.

'Just that mangy ginger one,' said Alex, suddenly attending to a wilting pot of mint. Alex didn't want Ferdie to see Princess-bloody-Tara. She didn't like the way he looked at her; all soppy smiles, his beautiful green eyes widening. And she especially didn't like the way his voice went all soft and gooey as if he was talking to a baby.

'Who's my pretty little fluffy-wuffy princess, then?' she'd overheard him say in the garden while stroking her one day. It'd made Alex want to vomit.

But it wasn't just the pet names she was concerned about. She'd come back from work to find Ferdie feeding her smoked salmon from his own fork. And then a few days later, she'd returned from the gym to find her lying on Ferdie's lap, pumping his legs with her claws, purring away. And just two nights ago, she'd got back from work early and caught them play wrestling on the sofa. *Her sofa.*

Alex headed back to the patio past Ferdie. He was standing on a chair peering through a pair of binoculars he used for bird-watching, scanning the neighbours' gardens.

'You can get arrested for that!' she called back.

'It's just that I haven't seen Princess all day.'

'Maybe she's been run over,' muttered Alex.

'Alex! That is *very* unkind.'

'Well,' mumbled Alex as she walked back into the house.

She left him searching for Princess Tara and picked up her supper tray. She winced. Only six months ago Ferdie's tray meant something very different to the one now on her lap. She pushed the thought away. Perhaps she was going mad. Perhaps Ferdie was right; it was love at first sight. But as much as she tried to recall the moment six months ago, she couldn't. All she could remember was another night of drinking too many cheap alcopops, dancing with men in bad taste outfits and vaguely racist Afro wigs and feeling too old and tired. She'd gone to the toilet, then the bar and when she returned to the dance floor her friends had disappeared. So she'd simply gone too. There had been no thunder and lightning, no butterflies fluttering, no weak at the knees moment. She certainly couldn't remember him coming home with her.

But perhaps Ferdie was right; she'd been too drunk to remember their first meeting. It wasn't as if it had never happened before. A couple of years ago, she'd woken with the birds at dawn, slumped on her front doorstep, unable to recall how she'd made the journey home from a Christmas party. Perhaps her sister was right? She should just be happy. She shouldn't question the fact that he was perfect. How could you complain about someone being too handsome, too tidy, too helpful and too thoughtful? Ferdie did everything. He cooked and cleaned. Not just token Hoovering but he actually cleaned; the floors, the toilet, wiped down the kitchen cupboards. He even rinsed the skirting boards twice a week.

I remember getting dusty as I walked past. It's not a good look, he'd told her when she found him on his hands and knees at 7am in the morning. *And it made me sneeze. Just as well as I love to clean!* Over and over again, she'd wondered how it had happened. Could you just will something to happen? If you wished for something enough times, then would it come true?

One disastrous date after another, she'd sit on the sofa with Ferdie curled up on her lap, his silky black paws resting on her knees. And she would tell him all about the man with the bad breath who spat every time he pronounced a 'th'; the builder who didn't ask her one single question all night, except her age, and then threw down a £50 note saying he only dated women under 30; the comb-over accountant who took long, lustful glances at every woman who walked by; the lawyer who groped her under the dinner table, his dogged hand eventually knocking her wine all over her; the recently divorced friend of a cousin who broke down, his tears dripping into his prawn cocktail. Ferdie had been an excellent listener, a listener like no other. He never once interrupted or yawned. He just let her talk. And after every disastrous date, she'd say the same thing: *I wish you could be my boyfriend, Ferdie. You'd make a fantastic boyfriend. You're clever, playful, affectionate, housetrained and handsome.* So handsome. She was right. He had the most beautiful face she'd ever seen. It was open and kind with a hint of mischievousness behind his green eyes. What she did remember was this: after the disco diva night, she'd cuddled up with him in bed and said, why can't I have someone like you, *Ferdie?* And when she awoke, Ferdie the cat was no longer next to her, purring. Instead, it was Ferdie the man, snoring.

A year after Ferdie moved in, he moved out. She'd caught him in bed with her after coming home early to prepare a surprise anniversary chicken supper. It was her all right. The grey hair had been replaced with long blonde tresses. But she'd recognise those amber eyes anywhere. She'd told him to get out and find some other sucker to scrounge off. And then a few weeks later, she made an appointment with Battersea Dogs Home. She'd find herself a handsome, strong but gentle Rottweiler perhaps, or even a Staffie-cross, though she imagined it may sport tattoos. But on second thoughts she could live with a couple of tattoos. After all it is temperament that really matters and everyone knows that dogs are far more loyal than cats.

---ooOoo---

FRIENDS AND STRANGERS

Jacqueline Summer

It had been one of those piercingly bright, short November afternoons. After the class Josie peers out into the fast darkening sky. It seems strange to have the builders walk back and forth at eye level just across the street. She can remember the churn and hum of the concrete mixers two months ago when they were putting in the foundations. Recently, the tock tock tock of the roof joists going up has penetrated her classes daily.

    Josie notices a builder pause in his work, in that moment she sees hands worn and swollen, one clutching a hammer. With his free hand against his lower back, he straightens stiffly and calls over to a younger man in yellow. A brief interchange punctuated by laughter: his, a low growl, the other man's higher with the forced glee of youth. The first man turns back to his task, but seems distracted by the opalescent hues of yellow, rose and blue glimpsed through the ribs of the roof.

    Josie senses his tiredness, his aches. He's probably been at work since 7am, she thinks, and he must be in his late fifties, early sixties. She packs away the student's assignments, spare hand-outs, pens. Outside she breathes in the swiftly cooling air, breathes it out with a sigh. The sky is clear ultramarine, a presage of frost.

    On the way to the station Josie's thoughts are filled with the builder. What must it be like to have worked for forty years using the muscles and sinews of your body like a workhorse? Still, there must be something satisfying about working as a group to form a structure from foundations to roof. To see it completed and in use. She reins in her thoughts. 'I'm probably seeing it through rose-coloured spectacles.'

He drains the last swill of beer and gazes, unseeing at the foam stained glass on the sticky table. How many was that? Four, five? He's lost count. He knows it is more than enough and yet how can he contemplate going home?

Mick is lulled by the warmth of the pub, the babble of conversation going on around him. It had been a long day, his hands throb from hammering and his back aches. He still can't quite believe what had just happened.

'Mick, need a word'.

He'd followed his foreman to the site 'office', a green portacabin sparsely furnished with a worn desk, two black plastic chairs stained with white paint and a small battered filing cabinet. The smell of damp overalls and rancid coffee dregs permeated the stuffy space, which was heated by two electric bars over the doorway. George offered him a seat, but Mick remained standing.

'Building's coming along' stated George obviously.

'Yeah, just the upper frames to go in then we can start on the interior fit'.

'Hmm, that's what I wanted to talk to you about. The company's losing money over this project. They've decided to bring in some jobbing builders for the fit, to economise with the finish.'

Mick's heart sank, not another cheap, tacky job. He longed for the days when his carpentry skills had been properly appreciated.

'Thing is, Mick, you're so skilled and, because of that, you cost the company. We don't need that kind of 'Rolls Royce' job now. What they want is cheap and cheerful. The jobbers and the lad can do it. I'm afraid we're going to have to let you go, mate. I'm sorry.' George turned away, shuffled papers on the desk, opened a cabinet drawer.

Mick knew George couldn't face him; they had been mates for thirty years. In the early days, they'd looked out for one another putting a word in here and there, to get one another work. But George had done better for himself. He had a brain, had gone to night school.

Mick looked down at his swollen hands in despair. How would he put food on the table, heat the house? There'd be no Christmas presents for the grandkids. How would he break it to Tracey?

He had his pride though. He straightened up, 'So, you're firing me George' he said looking his old friend in the eye. Before George, open-mouthed with dismay, could reply, Mick strode out banging the door hard enough to shake the whole portacabin.

'Heard it through the grapevine, Honey, Honey, no longer would you be my baa-by' smooches the juke box, bringing Mick back to his present surroundings. He notices the place has filled up now; kids from the art college across the road, talking loudly, shrieking with laughter, office workers standing around in cheap Next suits, one hand in a pocket, sipping lager.

Outside it has gone dark and bitterly cold. The force of freezing air hits his lungs, Mick coughs, pulls up the collar of his dusty jacket and heads towards the station unsteadily.

A crashing sound precedes the station master's announcement: 'We apologise for the delay to the 16.25 service to Dover and Canterbury West. The train is now expected at 17.15. The late running of this service is due to a fatality on the line. We apologise for any inconvenience this may cause'. Crunch, whine.

Tutting, sighing and much perusal of watches follows. Josie stamps her feet to keep warm. She wonders to what depths the person had sunk, to throw themselves under the wheels of an oncoming train. Her own petty miseries – Gary ending their relationship so soon after she'd moved to the area, her lack of friends – seem insignificant in comparison.

After the initial shock, the late running of the train seems to have caused a stir of wartime gaiety amongst stranded passengers. 'This is the third time this week my train's been delayed. I won't get home till after 7...'

'Too bad', commiserates an American accent. 'This is our first time travelling by train in the UK'.

'Not a very good first experience, then. Where are you from?'

Surprised at their lack of compassion, Josie's own eyes well up with tears, though she's not sure whether they are for the suicide victim, the train driver, or herself? She opens her felt bag, appliquéd with pink and white roses, to seek out a tissue and mistakenly releases one handle. The contents: make-up bag, diary, pens, board markers her purse bursting open, all fall to the platform. Rolling away across the greasy surface towards the stairs, she sees Damian's beautiful carved egg.

Josie runs after it just in time to witness a pair of familiar hands trap the wooden egg right on the brink of the flight of concrete steps. Mick emerges grinning, holding his catch aloft.

'Howzat!' he laughs infectiously. Josie notices his twinkling blue eyes and giggles.

'Oh thank you, thank you so much. Wait! I have to pick up the rest of my stuff...'

Mick follows her to the clutch of commuters who have gathered Josie's belongings. She expresses her gratitude effusively and turns to Mick.

'Let me buy you a coffee to thank you for your kindness.'

'I could do with a coffee', he agrees.

They enter the seething café, overfilled with travellers reading, but not buying, papers and magazines, while others merely shelter from the biting cold.

By the time Josie has bought two large lattes, Mick has managed to find space at a small table wedged in next to the cold drinks fridge. The fridge hums loudly. They move empty cups aside. Mick takes the egg from his pocket and places it gently between them on the sugary, cup-ringed table.

'Lovely piece of oak. Did you carve it?'

'Me? No, oh no. A student did. He's only seventeen, has lots of problems, but when it comes to working with wood he's a genius.'

'Needs a lot of determination – oak – how long did it take him?'

'He was working on it for about three weeks. But been absent now for two. I was going to take it round to his home at the weekend'. Imagine, if you hadn't saved it, the egg would have bounced down all those stairs. I wouldn't have been able to face Damian.' Josie pauses – an awkward silence intervenes.

'What do you do? I mean for a living.'

'I'm an art teacher at the local college, just across the street from the site where you work.'

Mick raises his eyebrows quizzically. 'How do you know where I worked?'

'You and your assistant have been on the same level as my classroom for some time now.'

Mick smiles, 'I didn't know we were being watched!'

They are interrupted by an electronic voice. 'We apologise for the delay to the 16.25 service to Dover and Canterbury West. The train is now due at 17.30. '

Josie glances at her watch, looks enquiringly at Mick.

'Worked?'

'Been laid off, that's all' replies Mick frowning into his cup. Then swiftly changing the subject he asks: 'Have you been at the college long?'

'Just since September. I moved down here in August to live with my boyfriend. He dumped me fourteen days ago.'

'Tough. How're you doing?'

'Not too well, actually. All my friends live in Birmingham. Life's all work and no play, right now.' Why am I telling him all this personal stuff? I've only just met him. I suppose he reminds me of Dad. Her throat constricts and she coughs slightly to clear it. It's her turn to change the subject:

'So, what're you going to do now?'

'Who's going to want to pay Master Carpenter rates to a slow, arthritic old man like me?' Mick says self mockingly.

Josie is concerned, her forehead wrinkles and she asks seriously; 'But it's Christmas in a few weeks, how are you going to manage?'

Mick's jaw tightens grimly. 'We'll manage. We always do'.

I've put my foot in it now, she thinks, and then naively states, a little too brightly, 'You seem to know a lot about wood'.

'Well, I know a thing or two. Oak's a very hard wood, tight grained – to form an egg like this from a block- takes someone with grit, someone who loves wood, too.' While he's talking Mick picks up the egg, moves it around his hands, enjoys the smooth finish, nods in approval.

'The train now arriving at Platform 2 is the delayed 16.25 to Dover and Canterbury West. The train will divide here make sure you are travelling in the correct part of the train...'

'So what will you do about your boyfriend?' risks Mick.

'Ex' she replies heavily. Now Josie looks stern as she scoops the egg into her bag, gathers hat and gloves. She takes a deep breath, looks directly at Mick and announces, half to herself 'I'm going to put my energies into making new friends instead.'

Mick nods, rises stiffly, hand to lower back.

'What about you?' she asks.

'Oh, I'll ring my old mate, George, tomorrow. See if he knows where there's any work going. Thanks for the coffee.'

Mick shakes Josie's hand vigorously. It feels warm and rough to her, like crusty bread. 'Well, thanks again', she offers awkwardly. They separate to search for a space in their respective parts of the dividing train.

On the way to Dover, Mick thinks about Josie, wishes he'd had an understanding teacher like her when he'd been struggling at Staines Comp. He has no doubt she will soon have a full social life and the pain of losing her boyfriend will gradually ease. He looks out towards the darkness and is met by his own reflection in the window pane. Not a pretty sight he thinks and starts texting Tracey to explain his lateness.

Josie begins to warm up as she stands surrounded by weary

fellow travellers. She is struck by Mick's resilience and courage in the face of difficulty. In a rush of insight Josie realises Damian has similar qualities. Her thoughts are punctuated by a quacking sound. Looking at the screen of her phone she sees the name DAMIAN.

---ooOoo---

BUREAUPHOBIA

John Sussams

'Just deal with this, Hawkins,' said the Town Clerk, handing me a file. 'It's a straightforward non-payment case. Say we appreciate his point of view but The Law is The Law.'

I opened the file and read the first letter.

Dear Sir,

With reference to your exceedingly rude and offensive letter, you surely must realise that demanding money with menaces is a criminal offence. If you think I owe you money for services rendered, by all means send me an itemised invoice and I will see that it gets the attention it deserves. However, I should warn you that I am not aware of any service having been provided at all during the past twelve months. I recycle all my own rubbish. I do not use your library. I was not educated in your area, nor was my education paid for by any local authority in the whole of the UK. The potholes in the unlit road outside my house have not been repaired. This leaves the Police and the Fire Brigade, whose services I have not needed but readily admit I might need one day. Now, according to your figures, these account for only 13.2% of the total expenditure. Therefore, the maximum you are justified in asking for would be £145.75 and not the £1104.18 you are demanding. Incidentally, the 25% discount for not having a wife and 2.4 children should surely be 75%. So a fair bill would actually be £72.87.

Yours faithfully,

S E Nex

Our reply, known to us as 'Letter B' and addressed to a Mr S F Nex had been returned unopened and marked 'NOT KNOWN AT THIS ADDRESS'.

'What do you want me to do? Serve a writ?' I asked.

'Yes, if you have to, but try to speak to him first. Make him see reason.'

'Well, I'll try,' I said, 'but he's obviously a nutter with a bee in his bonnet. Looney-Left, I shouldn't wonder. Can't pay, won't pay. I know the type. Can't we get someone from Social Services to do the necessary? They're better at it than I am.'

'No, Hawkins. They've got enough on their plate without serving writs.'

'Oh, all right. But I think I'd better change into some scruffy clothes or, at least, put on an anorak. They are very suspicious of men in suits, these nutters.'

I located the Nex residence in the village of Hogweed. It was the last house on a road leading to nowhere. It was surrounded by a high and very prickly hedge in the middle of which was a tall gate. On the gate there were two notices.

One read:
    NO JEHOVAH'S WITNESSES
    NO DOUBLE-GLAZING SALESMEN
    NO OFFICIALS OF ANY KIND
    NO JUNK MAIL

The other one read:
    BEWARE OF THE LEOPARD

Oh my God, I thought, we've got a right one here.

The gate was bolted on the inside but I managed to reach the bolt and let myself in. The front door was reached by a concrete path on either side of which vegetables were growing. Fancy growing vegetables in the front garden, I thought. But, then again, why not? I rang the bell.

'Who is that and what do you want?' The voice came from a hidden microphone. I thought it was slightly unusual for a small house such as this was, to have an entryphone system. But, then again, why not?

'My name is Jim Hawkins and I want to talk to you.'

'What about?'

'Your leopard.'

'I don't have a leopard,' said the voice.

'That's what I want to talk about,' I said, inspired. 'The leopard which you don't have.'

'In that case, I suggest that you bugger off now, before I open the leopard's cage and let him tear you to pieces.'

'Do you have a licence for this hypothetical leopard?'

'Just a minute,' said the voice. There was a scuffling noise behind the door and the sound of a chain being unfastened. The door was opened and S E Nex stood there, smiling. He was oldish, in his late fifties or early sixties, tall, clean-shaven, with piercing blue eyes and thinning grey hair. He wore grey trousers and a red and green checked shirt.

'Of course I have a licence – a hypothetical licence. Now what do you really want?' he asked.

'I represent the Council,' I said.

'Bloody hell!' said S E Nex. Then, recovering his composure, 'Well, bully for you! I represent God.'

'No, but seriously, you will have to pay your Council Tax. Otherwise they can take you to court and force you to pay. Or issue a distraint order. And it'll cost more that way. And also there will be legal costs. You can't win. You could even go to prison. So why don't you just give me a cheque and we can consider the whole matter closed. Write to your MP. Write to *The Times*. Call a public meeting. Do what you like. But pay up first. It's not as if you were destitute, is it?'

'No, I am not destitute. But I do try to avoid all unnecessary expenditure. Pay as you go, that's my motto. "Neither a borrower nor a lender be." Shakespeare said that: *Hamlet* Act 1, Scene 3. Freedom of choice, that I also believe in, which means the freedom not to buy something you don't want. But you people from the Council, you have no idea what you are selling or to whom or what its value is. I've been round this loop three times already, with the gas people, with the electricity people, with the water people, about their fixed charges. Well, they all said I had an option. I could either pay or have the supply cut off. All I want is for you to cut off the supply of whatever it is you think you are supplying. Then I won't have to pay, will I?'

'But you didn't have your gas, electricity and water supplies cut off, did you? You bit on the bullet and paid, didn't you?'

'Let me show you something,' said S E Nex; and he led the way to his kitchen and pointed to an Aga cooker. 'Do you know what that is?' he asked.

'That's an Aga cooker.'

'Exactly. No gas for cooking, water or space heating. Now come this way.' He opened a door and (behold!) there was a small electric generator chugging away. 'Do you know what that is?'

'An electric generator. But surely it would be cheaper to buy electricity from the grid, wouldn't it.'

'Well, it might be. It would depend on how you do your costing, particularly if you use as little as I do. Anyway, it's a question of principle. People have willingly gone to the stake for the sake of their principles. So when the water company said that they would be installing water meters at vast cost., I knew what I had to do. Follow me.' He went out into the back garden and pointed at a manhole cover. 'Do you know what is under there?' he asked.

'A well?'

'You're not far off. Actually, it's my private reservoir – eight thousand gallons of fresh water. I filled it up before I told the water company to cut off the supply. I top it up as necessary with rainwater collected from the roof and filtered. Any surplus goes into my fishpond.'

'What about sewerage?'

'No problem! Those clever Swedes have invented a device which turns the waste matter into a nice dry powder, which you can use in the garden as fertiliser, and, as I pointed out in my letter, all my other refuse is recycled and used in the garden, to make compost, or to heat the greenhouse, or it may be sold as scrap. So … what do you think?'

'Well, obviously, I'm impressed, but, unfortunately, my hands are tied, and you'll still have to pay your Council Tax. You see, it doesn't work in the same way as gas and electricity and water. It works on the basis of robbing Peter to pay Paul. And you are Peter. You have to fork out lots of money so that, for the good of society, we can try to teach idiots to read and to write, so that layabouts can be housed, so that underage girls can have babies, so that the Police can arrest young hooligans that the courts can't deal with effectively, and who re-offend again and again and again …Yes, I know, it would be cheaper to shoot them all – but we are a democracy. We are a sharing, caring, Christian country, and, if you don't shell out a measly £1104.18, we'll bloody well lock you up and throw away the key. Do you get the message?'

'Well, said S E Nex, there's just one more thing I want to show you.' He led the way to the garage and opened the side door. Then he gave me an almighty shove, slammed the door from the outside and locked it.

I could hear scuffling and grunting noises and, in the gloom, I could make out two gleaming red eyes and a large, dark, feline shape moving very slowly towards me. Jesus Christ! I thought. It really is a leopard. Well, old son, this is it. I was petrified. What a way to go. The beast remained stationary but I could hear its breathing and smell its pungent, sweaty smell. I did not dare shout out but simply pressed up against the wall, feeling sick.

Suddenly a bright light was switched on and there was this

stuffed leopard being slowly winched back towards its corner. And there was this Tannoy speaker from which scuffling and grunting noises were being emitted. The door opened and I staggered out. Quite frankly, I felt a bit of a fool. I went back into the kitchen and there was S E Nex, relaxed, and smiling.

'I thought you might like a cup of tea,' he said.

'Yes,' I said, 'that would be most acceptable.'

'Oh, and by the way, 'I've made out a cheque in the sum of a measly £1104.18. I trust that will be all right.'

'Yes,' I said, 'that will be just fine.'

A ginger cat walked into the room, sniffed at me and rubbed itself against my left leg.

'I call him Frank Cooper, you know, after the marmalade. I was going to call him The Leopard, but he's such a friendly little fellow, that didn't seem quite right.'

---ooOoo---

WHAT A LOVELY CAR

Barrie Thompson

Both officers sat idly chatting about nothing in particular. They had been on duty since 0600 hours that morning.; it was now close to midday. Suddenly their peace and quiet was interrupted , sending both officers into action by their call sign being called out from the radio: **Bravo Romeo 1-9**, **Bravo Romeo 1-9**, whilst one officer picked up the handset, to answer, the other started the car, ready to move off.

Bravo Romeo 1-9 Proceed to 146 Edwin Road, I say again, 146 Edwin Road. Call of shouting in the street.

They didn't bother to put the 'Blues and Twos' on. It was Monday morning. Nothing ever happens on a Monday morning. As they turned into Edwin Road, coming in from the top end, they could see two men having one hell of a ding-dong in the middle of the road. Pulling up just short of the men, they noticed two women on the pavement outside a pair of semi-detached bungalows. One of the women was obviously crying; the older woman was trying to comfort the younger one; she had her arm round her. As the officers got out, both men stopped shouting at each other and waited for them to approach.

'What seems to be the trouble?' one said.

'Look what he's done to my new car,' came the reply from the older gentleman, nodding towards a young man in overalls, standing next to him.

Parked outside the nearest bungalow was an obviously brand-new, bright red 2.8-litre BMW Z4 sports car with the hood down. Walking over to the car, both officers stood and looked in amazement, surprise, and horror: the whole of the inside of the vehicle was full of wet readymade concrete nicely setting solid. They looked at each other, then back at the small group of people now on the pavement waiting for their comments.

It transpired that the young couple had recently returned from their honeymoon in Spain. The young husband had gone off to work early that morning. He drove a Ready-Mix concrete lorry for a firm in Sittingbourne. His second trip of the day took him past the end of his road along the A2. He decided to stop and have a cup of coffee with his new young wife – or anything else that might be on offer. She still had a couple of days off. The thought of what might be on offer made him smile to himself. Arriving home, he saw the red BMW sports car parked outside his house. Someone's got some money, he thought. Not knowing who the owner was he decided to park up and investigate.

Parking just a little way up past the sports car, he got out of his cab and walked back down towards the car and home. Walking up his driveway, intending to go around the back of the bungalow, he stopped in horror as he turned the rear corner. Looking through the kitchen window, he saw his new young bride with her arms around a young man, fondly holding him tight to her beautiful young body. That was enough to send any man over the top. His blood suddenly boiled. Who was this interloper that he had never seen before?

I'll teach him, he thought. He retraced his steps back to his lorry with its full load of ready-mixed concrete. His mind was racing with thoughts of what might have been happening or what his wife might be doing with this man. He jumped into his lorry backing it down the road in frustration and anger, towards the sports car, his blood-sugar levels reaching an all-time high. He stopped, got out, and activated the chute into the open car, then turned the handle to let lovely gooey wet concrete shoot into the car, filling it up to the brim. He switched off the concrete, replaced the chute and drove back up the road a little way, smiling to himself. That will teach them, he thought, as he waited to see what would happen when this stranger had finished with his wife.

Sure enough, a little later, out walked this young intruder (the one he had seen in the kitchen) walking down the driveway onto the pavement. The man stopped, bent, and tucked his right trouser-leg into his sock, then climbed onto a bike which had been leaning up against the hedge, and cycled off down the road towards the main A2.

He sat in horror for a few moments. He hadn't noticed the bike in his haste to get home and see his bride.

He jumped out of his cab, ran home and burst through the back door.

'Who was that?' he shouted at his wife.

'Oh, that was my young brother, Dave. You've never met him. He's only just arrived home on leave from the Army. He couldn't get to the wedding,' she replied.

'Whose is the red sports car?'

'Oh, that's Fred's next door. He's been waiting six months for it to be delivered. Isn't it lovely?' came the reply.

Desperately trying to keep a straight face, one of the officers suggested both men should inform their own home insurance company. Before driving off as quickly as possible, both broke into hysterical fits of laughter and drove straight back to the police station to tell everyone what the *999* call had been about, and to enter it into the *OB* (Occurrence Book), which would make good reading for months to come.

---ooOoo---

THE TRAMP

Alexander Tulloch

Nobody could remember the Accident and Emergency Department ever being so quiet on a Saturday night. There had been one or two of the usual cases requiring urgent treatment following some sort of domestic accident. And a few of the obligatory drunks had shown up, some of whom had made their own way to the hospital for treatment and others who had been brought in by the police, but that was about it. The department frequently resembled a battle field at weekends but on this occasion it was deathly quiet and looked so deserted that it prompted one of the duty doctors to comment sardonically "All quiet on the Western Front."

In place of the normal hectic to-ing and fro-ing, frantic telephoning to contact various medical specialists and nurses enjoying the thrill of mercy dashes down the corridors as they made every second count in order to save a life, a strange stillness pervaded the whole hospital wing. A couple of the nurses were taking advantage of what they were convinced would only be a brief respite to catch up on the hospital gossip and to tell each other who was 'seeing' whom. In one of the staff rest rooms a young doctor was grabbing the opportunity to read a couple of pages of a Dickens novel, a writer for whom he had a particular liking.

As the night wore on and the expected storm, which everyone was convinced would soon break to shatter the prevailing calm, failed to arrive, Dr. Jacobs closed his copy of "Oliver Twist", stood up, stretched and decided he would walk down the corridor and get himself another cup of the dreadful coffee dispensed by the department's newly acquired vending machine.

But he had not taken more than a couple of steps towards his intended destination when a nurse came up to him and informed him that an old man had been brought in after being found wandering about the hospital grounds in a confused state. "Oh well," he said to himself, "I didn't really fancy another cup of that awful gunge anyway … Let's have a look at him, then."

The old man was wheeled on a trolley into one of the observation cubicles and Dr. Jacobs followed him in, accompanied by the nurse.

"Can you tell me your name?" said the doctor, addressing the patient.

"The name's Bond – James Bond," came the reply

"Say again," said Dr Jacobs, thinking he had misheard him the first time.

"James Bond," repeated the old man. "And don't laugh. That really is my name. I'm seventy-six-year-old and have had the name longer than the other feller."

Doctor Jacobs could not help smiling as he looked at the decrepit old man who, by any standards, was just about as unlike his namesake as it was possible to be. Nobody could have failed to be struck by the irony of this poor old man, who resembled the archetypal tramp, having a name which conjured up images of suave virility and clean-cut sophistication.

"I think the first thing we'll do, nurse, is get his clothes off him and give him a bath," said the doctor after giving him an examination which revealed no injuries. "There's nothing wrong with me," said Mr Bond. "I don't know why I was brought here. I was looking for somewhere to sleep and must have wandered into in the hospital grounds. I suppose someone thought I'd been taken ill."

"Well, we can't take chances, can we?" replied Dr Jacobs. "You can go with the nurse now and she'll get you cleaned up and then we'll keep you in overnight for observation."

When the nurse had taken Mr Bond away Dr Jacobs went over to the reception desk and asked who had brought the old man in and why. He had not been able to find anything wrong with him and, in fact, had concluded that, considering Mr Bond's life style, he was in pretty good shape.

The girl on reception informed him that Mr Bond had been found by one of the nurses coming on night duty. She also said that when he was first admitted he was very confused; so confused in fact that she thought he was drunk. He hadn't got a clue where he was or what day it was and he hadn't even been able to tell anyone his name. When asked how old he was his only reply had been a glazed, blank stare.

"Strange," thought Dr Jacobs, "he was quite compos mentis with me and I saw him only a few minutes after reception. Oh, well, I'll have another look at him when he's had a bath," and off he went down the corridor to have the coffee he had promised himself earlier.

Another couple of chapters of "Oliver Twist" later Dr. Jacobs decided that it was pointless trying to read any more. Although his eyes had read the last few pages, his mind had not taken in a single word. He was puzzled by this old tramp and the more he tried not to think about him the more he seemed to intrude on his thoughts and his reading. "Why do I do this?" he asked himself. "I'd much rather have been a writer than a doctor. I'm a bit like Oliver Twist, I suppose, the way I keep asking for more. The difference is that he asked for more when he hadn't had enough and I ask for more when I've already had about as much as I can take."

Dr Jacobs was a voracious reader. He always had been. He sailed through medical school because of his uncanny ability to read voluminous text books and remember almost everything he had read. His tutors and fellow students alike were frequently astounded by the way in which he could reel off whole chunks of "Grays Anatomy" and other medical classics and they were equally surprised at his facility for instant recall. Where other students had to slave away, night after night, committing to memory chapters on pathology, haematology and God knows how many other weird and wonderful -ologies, Dr Jacobs needed to read them only once and all the detail was there, in his head, ready to emerge word for word whenever the occasion demanded.

But if reading medical text books was an integral part of his professional life, reading novels, particularly the classics, was his relaxation. He had acquired a liking for Hardy, the Brontes, Austen and Dickens, not to mention all the nineteenth century foreign authors he had added to his repertoire, while still at school and his passion for them had stayed with him. Now they had become a sort of refuge; a place where he could retreat to when he felt the need to escape from the relentless pressures of life as a hospital doctor.

When he was taking the last few gulps of coffee the nurse came back into the rest room and told Dr. Jacobs that the old man had been given a bath and was now in bed on one of the wards. As there were no other cases requiring his attention Dr Jacobs thought that he would take a stroll down to the ward to see how James Bond was settling in.

"How are you feeling now, Mr Bond?" he asked with practised solicitude.

"All right, Doctor," came the reply

The patient looked and smelled very different now. The whiff of stale body odours had been replaced by the more acceptable fragrance of the hospital's bulk-purchase, standard soap. His hair and beard were still as long and straggly, but now they also reflected the care and attention Nurse Winstanley had lavished on them with a brush and comb.

Doctor and patient talked for some ten minutes, or rather, the doctor asked questions for some ten minutes and James Bond replied. All the time he was talking to him, Dr Jacobs was trying not only to build up a case file of previous medical history etc. but also to assess his mental state. There seemed to be no sign of the "confusion" the girl on reception had reported. But it was during this conversation-cum-examination that Dr Jacobs began to experience a rather odd sensation. The more he talked to James Bond the more the doctor became aware that his patient reminded him of someone. At first he could not quite put his finger on who it was, but the feeling that he had seen or met this man somewhere before got stronger and stronger. Eventually it came to him. It was Fagin. The man in the bed talking to him was the spitting image of an illustration he had seen in some edition of "Oliver Twist" years ago, possibly from his childhood, when he had first been introduced to the Dickens story .

It was at this moment that the Doctor glanced at the tramp's bedside locker. On the top among the chewing gum, crumpled cigarette packets, bits of string and other detritus taken from his pockets lay a paperback copy of Ian Fleming's "Goldfinger."

"Is this yours?" said Dr. Jacobs, who could not resist the urge to pick the book up and flick through its pages.

"Yes, Doctor," said Mr Bond. "I've always been an avid reader. In fact you're talking to the original sauce-bottle label reader. I'll read anything: newspapers, novels, poems … anything you care to name."

"Really?" said the doctor, unable to conceal the pleasure he felt at having found a literary soul-mate. "And who is your favourite author?"

"Can't say, really," replied the old man, and then continued, "I suppose the easiest way to answer your question is to say that my favourite author is always the author of the book I last read. I've read most of the works of people like Dickens, Hardy and Tolstoy, but I can enjoy the more modern writers who write what you might call novels for 'light reading'. It's no exaggeration to say that I'll read whatever I can get my hands on. At the moment I'm reading all the Bond books. Nothing gives me greater pleasure than to find a comfortable doorway or park bench and settle down to a good read. I sometimes think I could have been a writer, but I never had the education. So instead of writing books I just read them. It helps me escape from reality. When I have an absorbing book in my hands I can get so deep into it that I don't feel the cold and don't even notice my hunger pangs."

Dr. Jacobs was now beginning to experience a certain sympathy for his patient. After all, the opportunity to actually talk to his patients did not present itself all that often, and when it did, it was very rare to meet someone who shared his interest in books.

"Excuse me, Doctor," said the tramp, suddenly changing the subject, "but would it be possible for me to have something to eat? I haven't eaten at all today, and I haven't had a square meal for a week."

"Dear me," came the reply, "is that so? Yes, of course, I'll see what I can do. The kitchens are closed now until breakfast, but I'm sure one of the nurses will be able to find you a cheese roll or a couple of sandwiches. I'll get her to make you a pot of tea as well. Now, getting back to why you were brought in here. Can you tell me anything about this dazed and confused state the nurse who found you and the nurse on reception said you were in? I can't see any sign of it. You seem to be quite bright and alert to me."

"Dazed and confused state? Who? Me? No idea what you mean. But it's an interesting philosophical point, isn't it?"

"How do you mean?"

"Well, if I was found in a confused state and had had some sort of memory blackout, I wouldn't know anything about it afterwards, would I?"

Dr. Jacobs decided that it was time to bring the discussion to a close. His parting smile told the tramp that this fine representative of the medical services had no real answer to the question he had just posed and so he thanked the doctor again for his help, but asked him not to forget the promised sandwiches and pot of tea.

Back at the reception desk Dr. Jacobs had just been informed that another accident case had been admitted. He was also informed that the police wanted to have a word with him about the old tramp in ward 7.

"Ah, Dr Jacobs, I presume," said a voice behind him. "I'm

Constable Smithers. What can you tell me about this man calling himself James Bond?"

"Er, not an awful lot, I'm afraid," replied the doctor. "He was brought in here in a confused state, but has no physical injuries and seems relatively hale and hearty. We're keeping him in over night for observation and he'll probably be discharged in the morning."

"Well," said the constable, "he's well known to us. He's a right rogue. He's pulled this stunt at other hospitals. First he pretends to be stoned out of his mind so that he gets taken into a hospital where he gets a warm bed for the night and a couple of meals. Oh, yes, and he always gives as his name the main character in the book he's reading at the time. When he's not reading he's thieving and generally living off his wits. But our main problem is that he has this band of local tearaways who do a lot of his dirty work for him. In fact, down at the station we call him 'Fagin'.

---ooOoo---

THE HERO

Alexander Tulloch

The Kent countryside was the perfect spot for the hospital. The wounded soldiers coming back from France could be taken straight from Folkestone to its warm wards, dry beds, soft sheets and angelic nurses. The horrors of the trenches and the dreadful, nightmarish world of explosions, mutilations and, for the lucky ones, instant death, could be left behind as the young men set off along the long road to rehabilitation.

At the beginning of the "War to end war" nobody had envisaged that there would be such a desperate need to convert some of the finest stately homes in England into hospitals where thousands upon thousands of that blighted generation could be nursed back to health. This is not to say that a full recovery was a possible or even feasible goal in every case and, in the context of that wholesale carnage and slaughter, being "nursed back to health" was a relative term. What it frequently meant was learning to cope with having no legs, only one arm or coming to the terms with the fact that you would never see the trees, the green fields or your sweetheart's face again. If the truth be told, only a small number of those who returned to England for medical treatment ever made a complete recovery. And the few who did were immediately shipped out again to run the same risks of being scythed by German machine-gunners as they had on their first posting.

The generals had assured everybody, from the government down, that the war would be over by Christmas. The British Tommy was the finest soldier in the world, led by the most intelligent, most highly trained and dedicated officer corps that any nation had produced in the history of warfare. If proof were needed of the

Army's invincibility, all one had to do was look at any school atlas and see just how much of the world was covered in red. Yes, that upstart Kaiser Bill had bitten off far more than he could chew in taking on Britain, her Empire and European allies and a brief campaign on the other side of the Channel would suffice to bring him to his Teutonic knees. Nobody entertained the slightest doubt that fighting for King and Country was an honourable thing to do and that victory was assured. All the recruitment posters persuaded the young men of military age that, if they joined up, they would not really be marching off to war, but merely taking advantage of the opportunity to make real men of themselves and return, covered in glory, to a hero's homecoming. Fathers throughout the land exhorted their sons to do their duty, little thinking, if they thought about it at all, that "doing their duty" frequently meant nothing more than stopping a German bullet.

Sir Randolph and Lady Beauchamps were appalled when they received the letter from the War Office informing them that their ancestral home was to be requisitioned and converted into a hospital for soldiers wounded in France. The house had been in Sir Randolph's family for generations and it seemed dashed unfair to him that he and his wife should be forced to spend the war living in their all too small *pied-à-terre* near Eton Square. The place simply was not big enough for entertaining and, as there were no servants' quarters, they would have to rely on finding a cook and maids who lived no more than a short tram-ride away. They did protest, of course, but it did no good. The country was at war and that was that. The government needed an ever-increasing stock of places to care for the wounded, the maimed and those who would remain permanently disfigured for the rest of their lives.

The Beauchamps had been enduring the privations of their Knightsbridge existence for some six months when, by an irony of war, they found themselves being driven through the grounds of their recently converted home in the Garden of England. Second Lieutenant Harry Beauchamps, their son, had been wounded in

France and shipped back to the military hospital. Details were sketchy, but as far as Sir Randolph could ascertain, the wounds were not considered life-threatening and he interpreted this as meaning that his son was not seriously wounded. Apparently Harry had been involved in some engagement with the Bosch and after several hours bitter fighting in which many were killed on both sides, the Kaiser's lot had pulled back and yielded some ten yards of ground to Harry's battalion. The only piece of hard news Sir Randolph and Lady Beauchamps received, in the form of official notification from the War Office, was that their son had been awarded a medal for the manner in which he had conducted himself in the face of danger on the battle field. The discovery that they had a hero for a son was reasonable compensation for having to surrender their beautiful home for the duration of the war.

When Sir Randolph and his wife walked through the main doors of the hospital an orderly at the make-shift reception desk informed them which ward they would find their son in. As they walked through what had once been their splendid dining room, they were horrified by the sights and sounds which greeted them. Grown men were sobbing and weeping, crying out in agony, writhing and groaning as they clutched their sides, stomachs or groins. There were men sitting in chairs staring vacantly at the bloodstained bandages protecting the stumps that remained after a leg (or, in some cases, both legs) had been amputated; others just sat and looked blankly into space while yet others bore no physical wounds but shook and twitched uncontrollably without the slightest idea of where they were or even who they were.

But the dreadful sights they saw in their dining room were no preparation for what they were to encounter when they entered their former drawing room. The sumptuous Persian carpet on which Sir Randolph had wrestled and played with Harry as a four-year-old had gone and their footsteps now echoed off the bare floor-boards as they walked over them. On one of the dozen or so beds which had replaced their beautiful, expensive furniture they saw their son, or, rather, what was left of him. Where his arms should have been there was nothing and one leg was encased in plaster and suspended at an angle of forty five degrees by some contraption hanging from the ceiling. If such a sight were not bad enough for loving parents to be met with, the most ominous sight for them both were the bandages covering their son's eyes. Sir Randolph and Lady Jayne just stood and stared at their beloved boy as if suffering from shell-shock themselves. For some reason their minds just could not cope with what their eyes were telling them. Lady Jayne, in particular, had difficulty in comprehending what was happening and her mind kept on throwing up images of former, happier times. All she could think of was that the last time she had stood on this spot she had been supervising the decoration of the Christmas tree before the guests arrived for the Beauchamps' customary lavish Christmas Eve dinner. The confusion in her mind was compounded by the way in which the groaning and moaning of the wounded men around her mingled with her memories of the festive laughter of not so long ago.

They had been standing by their son's bed for no more than a couple of minutes when a nurse approached them and informed them that the doctor would welcome the opportunity of a chat with them in his office. The "office" turned out to be the Beauchamps' former breakfast room.

The doctor, a colonel in the Royal Army Medical Corps, greeted Sir Randolph and Lady Jayne politely but he was forced to dispense with the customary platitudes which he was in the habit of uttering when faced with traumatised parents. Sir Randolph's forthright manner cut right through the conventional formalities as he immediately launched into the offensive: "What the devil's going on here? I was told that my son's wounds weren't life-threatening."

"They're not," replied the colonel. "Your son will live."

"My son? ...Live? That's not my son out there. My son is an athlete ... rowed for Cambridge and all that......how can you say he'll live? ... what kind of a life will he have in that state?"

"Sir Randolph," said the colonel, trying to take some of the heat out of the conversation, "I have seen worse cases than your son. At least he has come back to you. The war is over for him. In a few months you'll be able to take him home."

The irony of the remark went unnoticed as Sir Randolph and Lady Beauchamps were in too great a state of shock to notice it and the RAMC colonel was unaware of the provenance of the house which now served as his hospital.

"The bandages," said Lady Jayne, who until now had been sitting quite still, in a scarcely audible whisper. "Why are his eyes covered by those bandages?"

"Well," began the colonel, hesitantly, "I'm afraid there has been considerable damage to your son's eyes. We can't be absolutely sure yet, but you should prepare yourselves for the possibility that your son may be blind."

The colonel obviously thought that he should get all the bad news over in one fell swoop and so, before Sir Randolph or Lady Jayne could say anything more, he added,

"And I must ask you if you have any other children."

"No," replied Lady Jayne, "Harry is our one and only."

But before she had finished her reply her eyes flashed as some primeval maternal instinct informed her of the doctor's purpose in asking that question. Her gasp of dismay anticipated his next statement.

"Then I'm sorry to have to tell you that your son has other wounds which mean that you will never have any grandchildren."

Sir Randolph's and Lady Jayne's world was falling apart. Sir Randolph had always taken it for granted that when he retired his son would take over as owner and Managing Director of the family munitions factory and that he, in turn, would hand it down to his son when the time came. Lady Jayne had more basic needs; she had always looked forward to having grandchildren. She simply wanted to experience the joy of watching them grow up and to build her life around theirs. Neither ambition would be realised now.

"But at least you can take comfort from the fact that your son is a war hero."

This was not the right thing to say or the right time to say it. Sir Randolph felt his anger and frustration boiling to the surface at the same time as he was aware of his jingoistic patriotism ebbing away.

"What bloody good is being a war hero? He's only twenty-four years old … what kind of future has he got now? Oh, yes, there'll be lots of flag waving and military bands at the victory parade. But what then? You know as well as I do, Colonel, that within months if not weeks of the armistice cripples like Harry will be forgotten. And who'll look after him when my wife and I are no longer here? I don't mind admitting that, right now, I wish he'd had a bit more of the coward in him. I don't mean he should have fled the field of battle, but if he'd been a bit less enthusiastic about fighting the Bosch he might have come home in one piece.'

"I'm very sorry, Sir Randolph," replied the colonel, directing his gaze to the floor. "There really is nothing more I can say. Of course, we will help your son all we can, and do, please, feel free to come and visit him as often as you like."

As they emerged from the hospital, Sir Randolph and Lady Jayne did not say a word to each other. In stunned silence they slowly walked down the half dozen or so steps and headed to where their chauffeur was waiting for them with the Rolls.

On "their" lawn they could see convalescent soldiers enjoying the last half hour of the warm spring sunshine as they practised walking on crutches or learned how to manoeuvre a bath chair. Lady Jayne looked at them and could not help admitting to herself that she felt more than just a little resentment towards those who still had arms and legs or could see. Her very soul was caught in a maelstrom of violent emotions; she wanted to stay at her son's side and stroke his golden hair, but at the same time she was desperate to flee from what had been transformed into her own personal torture chamber. In her mind fond memories of yesteryear vied with the recent images of Hell and she could already sense that there would be no escape from her torment until the final relief that awaits us all.

But the only thought running through Sir Randolph's head was that he had never seen "his" garden looking so beautiful. He could not remember ever having seen such a wonderful display of daffodils as the one which was spread out before him on that glorious April evening.

---ooOoo---

TICKET OUT OF POOLE

Mike Umbers

'No one could be bored sailing,' he said, his eyes sparkling. 'Every wave is different!' I couldn't believe it: he was like all the others. Of course the waves are different, but the discomforts are the same, getting your feet wet, having your hair blown about, breaking your nails …I was born in Poole, live and work in Poole, and every boy I ever meet in Poole wants to be a sailor! I looked at Paul across the table; I didn't say what I thought – no point in parting with a guy until you have to, especially a rich guy. He didn't even notice my reaction. Just kept on about the wind and the waves. He was even squandering his obviously considerable wealth on having a boat built!

The subject hadn't come up before. We'd met at a party, gone on to the Criterion (none of my friends could afford the Criterion), gone back to his flat overlooking the harbour, slept together (he was very good at that), and now we were breakfasting by the picture window. I've *never* slept with a man on a first date, but we'd really clicked. Now the dreadful truth – he was a sailor.

We got closer though, despite that. More meals in smart places; more nights at his flat; sailing wasn't mentioned. Then a text: 'To Plymouth to boatbuilder tomorrow. Come too?' He was obviously suggesting a weekend in a hotel. I didn't mind that (he was very good at that). It would be a good hotel, and I like good hotels, a good hotel is my sort of place. I texted 'Can do. Ready 3.00pm.'
Mother came out too when he collected me She was astonished I'd agreed to go off with a yachtsman. She knew why when she saw the car.

The Hotel matched expectations. Paul had stayed before. With other girls? I didn't care, I had him this time. We dined well, raided the drinks fridge and enjoyed the evening and night together. Breakfast was room service, you just get up, shower, and eat on the balcony. Boats part of the view OK, but I know his new boat will take over his life.

Next day we walked to Saunders Boatyard. Old Mr Saunders greeted us; I loved his Devon burr. He shook hands courteously and offered to show me the yard while Paul talked to young Mr Saunders, his great-nephew. We started at the wood shed, open-sided, planks neatly stacked. It seems you use different woods for different purposes, and they are stored for years to 'condition'. He pulled lengths out for me to admire, running his hand along the grain. 'There's pieces here,' he said, 'from my brother's time.' Apparently his brother, young Mr Saunders' grandfather, had founded the firm. Now young Mr Saunders ('Gearge', he called him) ran it. He showed me lathes and planing machines and old hand tools with infectious enthusiasm. I could not believe I would enjoy looking at a workshop.

Paul and George Saunders joined us. He took us to where Paul's boat was building. It was beautiful, I had to admit it was beautiful. Not so big as I'd expected, but fitted out with shower and toilet, kitchen ('galley' they called it), a bedroom with two bunks that pulled across into one big one – I liked that, but didn't comment and tried not to meet Paul's eye in case a smirk gave offence. The cabin had a table, bench seats…it was perfect; I'd have loved it if the damned thing never had to go on the water. Now I discovered Paul had designed her, and the Saunders were really impressed with his ideas, and enjoying building it for him.

Then rain set in and we went to the Cinema; no mention of hiring a boat thank God. And another leisurely meal and early night, early to bed anyway… Sunday was thoroughly wet, but it didn't matter, we drove home with the top up which I prefer anyway to getting my hair blown. I emailed thanks to Paul and texted them again next day from the office.

Then he went abroad on a business trip. Paul worked for his father's firm. They manufactured plastic shapes in Southampton but his parents lived in Jersey and Paul ran the factory from Poole. I heard nothing for days, and I missed him. Suppose he asked me to move in with him. Would I? He was fun and rich, but somehow lacking in … *empathy*. He was cold inside, generous with money because he had a lot, but self-centred. He must have realised I was never going to crew his new yacht, my interest in that was confined to the double bed. It was a puzzle to analyse my feelings.

Then he texted: 'Back to Plymouth Friday. Need help. Please come.' Why my help? What had happened? I rang but no reply so I left a message to say I couldn't be ready until five o'clock, but I'd come. Then I was out, so he left a curt message: 'Pick u up 5.'

'Whatever is it, Paul? Why are we going back so soon?'

He spoke like a record, unemotionally, controlling himself. 'A fire. At the Yard. Everything gone!' 'Paul! That's terrible. Not your lovely boat – ?' 'That's gone, but so's the Yard, the machinery, everything. George says his uncle is suicidal. I felt I had to go and I wanted you there too.' The astonishing thing, I realised, was that it wasn't the boat, it was two lovely men whose heart was in their Yard and their craft. 'I'm glad you asked me. I don't know what I can do but I'm glad. That poor old man – those lengths of wood – he was stroking them, Paul, like they were alive. Have they gone?' 'I guess so. George said it's all gone, he apologised for my boat, but the boat's insured, to hell with the boat. Then he said about his uncle. I had to come Gemma.'

We walked to the Yard next morning. The office hut was still there unharmed by the fire and George was waiting. He led us round the back. It was devastation: the woodstore and the two nearly completed boats had burnt so hot the roof above had collapsed, the two workshops were a tangle of metal, the smell was terrible. 'How did it start?' asked Paul. George Saunders shrugged his shoulders. 'They're still investigating.' Then he added angrily 'But they're suspicious, it could be an insurance job. 'Deliberate, you mean?' George laughed harshly. 'They should see my Uncle. Can you believe we'd do that? This yard was his life – I doubt he'll survive it.' We walked back to the office. 'Last year he lost his wife,' he told me, 'He had this then, now he hasn't anything.'

The old man, formerly so courteous, didn't even look up when we went inside. Paul said 'They'll find it was accidental – we know it has to be – the Insurance'll pay up, it's a set-back, but not the end surely?' 'It's not so simple. Money will buy a new shed, new tools, it'll buy wood, but not weathered wood – you can't insure that for its true value. And the lads have to be paid even when we can't give them work – they'll have to move on, they're craftsmen, they'll get jobs. No, we can't carry on, we both know that.' I saw Paul squeeze the old man's hands; it was a gesture of comfort and I realised how wrong I had been about his 'empathy'.

A wild thought came to me. Did I dare? They needed shocking into action. I hit the top of the desk with a clenched hand. 'You're too ready to give up,' I said, rather too loudly in my nervousness; I moderated my voice. 'Of course you can buy weathered wood. It'll just cost more. You can solve this Paul – buy a share in the Company! Be a sleeping partner if you like, or move here and join them. You told me once you envied craftsmen who worked with their hands, not like your plastics factory. ' He had said something like that. At the very least he might lend them money. 'And you still want a boat. So they've got their first order. The office is still here, the plans and contacts. You can afford it Paul, put money into Saunders Boat Yard.' I was breathless, passionate. Paul stared at me. Old Mr Saunders had turned to look at me astonished, young Mr Saunders was gripping the back of the chair in front of him, and I felt the tension. What was Paul going to say? I'd known him barely three months, we only had a physical relationship. Who was I to tell him what to do with his money?

There was a silence. I knew not to spoil the effect by saying more. Paul said slowly 'I'll need to see the books.' I gasped. 'And I'll need to phone my Father,' he went on thoughtfully. He stood up and turned to George Saunders. 'Gemma might have an idea. Will extra money keep you in business?' 'If there's enough of it. I'll work twenty hours a day – your boat first. I'll do it for him – ' he gestured to the old man who was looking up with a new light in his eyes. 'We buy Jameson's,' he said, his voice strained and hoarse. 'Gearge, we buy Jameson's.' George looked at him in astonishment. 'He's right!' he exclaimed. 'He's bloody right. Sorry miss! He's right of course. Sam Jameson's retiring, no sons to carry on.' The old man spoke again: 'And we'll do our own hulls.' 'Of course,' said George. 'We sub-contract the fibre-glass hulls,' he explained, 'but we could do it ourselves, with two yards, take on more staff.' His voice trailed off; was he going too far ahead? Was the young gentleman really that interested in their problem, or his girlfriend's solution? But by now I knew: a light had come on in Paul's eye – it was the light of a helmsman steering for the far horizon! 'I'm in that line now,' said Paul slowly, 'plastics, and moulding. Got contacts – it might work.'

They talked for an hour. Paul made no promises aloud but he phoned his father, then they talked to Sam Jameson, then Paul inspected files and phoned his father again, but he didn't open up and I was left to myself, still wondering what I'd started or if I'd done the right thing. I knew that night in bed in the Hotel. The sex was different. I'd always thought him good at it, but it was a performance, a clever performance, to impress with his prowess. That night was different. He was making love. Afterwards we lay and touched, and he said –

"Can you remember what you said, Paul? I've let you read my Journal, how we met. It was different that night wasn't it? And like I'd seen a new side of you, you saw a new side of me when I shouted at you all. I'd thought you a spoiled stud, a playboy yachtsman! And you'd thought me a shallow materialistic gold-digger. And you'd wanted a crew! You proposed next morning at breakfast and took me straight home to speak to Mother and the following weekend to Jersey to your family, and it was a whirlwind! I don't know whether we talked more

about boat-building or about weddings! But we did go house-hunting in Plymouth – you were my ticket out of Poole! You even got me to love your boat. You called her ' Gemma' but I made it 'Gemma 2' because the first 'Gemma' was the boat that never went to sea, the boat that brought us together. But I still prefer boats off the water!"

---ooOoo---

FLIGHT

Mike Umbers

'Oh, I have slipped the surly bonds of earth ...
Put out my hand, and touched the face of God.'

What utter balls! If I hear that poem read at one more funeral I shall go outside and puke. Mrs Anderson wanted me to read it for Peter but I got out of it by saying it was the Wing Commander's prerogative; it was his party piece and he did it very well. If I had done it I'd have heard Peter's mocking voice behind me and I'd have dissolved into tears or laughter – and broken down. It's from a poem called Ecstasy by someone called John Magee, and he was killed too, at the same age as Peter, just 19, and it was published in *The Daily Telegraph*, and then all the families wanted it. Actually I didn't cry at all at the funeral, though I expected to, especially when the Boss made that little pause he always made in the sixth line as if he was overcome, the old fake. Mrs Anderson didn't cry, so how could I? She looked very old and shrunken, not at all as I remember her when I used to visit her and Peter during the school holidays. After the Service in the Station Chapel, when we all came out and stood around, she shook my hand without a word and got in her car, and was driven away to the empty Manor House with all Peter's personal gear in the boot, and I guessed I'd never see her again. I went back to our bunk in the Mess Annexe where his bed was stripped and his cupboard and drawers emptied, and I threw myself on his bare mattress and sobbed.

We scrambled that night. I was glad; I needed action, and adrenalin proved stronger even than grief. I hoped not to come back, but of course I did, I always did, though my flying got crazier and my kills mounted. I even wondered if Peter was up there with me, his flying skills joined to mine; I shouted to him sometimes, and caught myself listening as if I was expecting an answer.

After the War, with three medals and an artificial knee, I took up my deferred place at Trinity. We were both to have gone up: Peter was the first in his family to go to University and had got an Exhibition at Emmanuel worth £20 a term which his family didn't need, but I only got a Place and that was more the result of having had a grandfather and a father (who *could* have done with the money) at the College. They were strong on family connections then, but of course nowadays it would be called nepotism and you'd be rejected on principle! The Cambridge I went up to in the Autumn of '45 was not the Cambridge my father knew, nor the one my son found when he went up last year. For one thing, many of us then were in our mid-20's. We had fought a war, we had lost friends and, more than that, we needed to catch up on the youth we had missed. That didn't make us wild party-goers; on the contrary, it made us want to get the delayed qualification we needed to start earning a proper living at last, and settling down into family life. The mood was sober and hard-working and the difference between us and the callow sixth-formers who'd missed the War and arrived and studied alongside us could not have been greater.

In the very nature of things, the intense grief for Peter died away, especially when I was no longer flying. But I still missed him intensely from time to time, mainly when I wanted to share some triumph or tragedy with a soul-mate. I had lost half of myself at an age when I didn't fully know myself. We had both realised even before we left School that being in different Cambridge Colleges, and on opposite sides of town too, and reading different subjects, would stop the daily intimacy we had shared since our Housemaster had allotted us as nervous new boys to the same dorm and study for no better reason than that our names both began with 'A'. Then in our last year there as Seniors, the War had dominated our thoughts and we had hardly discussed a future beyond it; we were mad keen to pass selection and qualify as fighter pilots – as we did, together. And again, it was because of that shared capital 'A' that we were posted to the same Unit, and after a brief leave we reported to 251 Squadron at Hawkinge near Folkestone on the South coast, and dropped our kit down in the same room in the Mess.

Flying was the most concentrated and intense experience I had ever had:
'*I've chased the shouting wind along, and flung*
My eager craft through footless halls of air…'
That damned poem again! We used to quote those lines to each other. It was later, when the funerals started, that we all (except for the Wing Commander) began to see through them: Magee's sky had no enemy planes coming towards you, spouting fire. He never wet his pants. Peter would have been horrified to know his mother wanted that cheesy rubbish read at his funeral.

I met Elaine soon after coming down and we married the following Autumn. I invited Mrs Anderson of course – I had kept up a feeble correspondence with her – but she refused as I expected. I kept her informed when Peter was born and then Mark, but I didn't make too much of it because it merely emphasised her loneliness; our correspondence dwindled to a 'Christmas letter'. She was in her nineties when she died – we had a formal letter from her Solicitor. I wasn't at her funeral – I had to drive to York on a business trip – but I couldn't get them out of my thoughts, and I felt so close to Peter that I spoke to him in the car and told him things. I even whispered those damned lines:
'*I've topped the wind-swept heights with easy grace,*
Where never lark nor even eagle flew….'
I reminded him of the times I had stayed with them in the school holidays; memories came flooding back and I shared them aloud in an empty car.

Peter's father had been a manufacturer of something profitable – wire or nails or whatever – and had made a pile and bought a country estate and promptly died. I never met him. Mother and son were already very close and now became closer. Peter came once to stay with me, but the contrast with my family embarrassed me – my parents were busy still with earning a living, our uninteresting suburban house had little to offer two active boys, and in any case I knew Mrs Anderson would be missing him. I suggested we always went to him for our summer holiday visit, and he was pleased; we were so close we could discuss a personal issue like that together without embarrassment. I could tell Peter things I have never told Elaine: we shared completely the comedy and angst of teenage youth. He even saw my poetry which she has never done. Yet he never showed me his Journal – that was the only reservation between us, and I respected it, and certainly didn't resent it.

It was three weeks after Mrs Anderson's funeral that a second letter came from the Solicitor. I was to meet him at their London Office to discuss her Will. I knew she had sold up and moved to a sheltered flat in Brighton: I now found she had left it to me, with its contents, and money beside. It was a life-changing legacy. When Probate came through Elaine and I left the boys with friends for the weekend and drove to Brighton. We stayed in a hotel – suddenly money was not an issue! Next morning we visited our property; we spent the day there and explored it together. Elaine was peering into drawers and cupboards, wondering how and where to make a start. She came into the bedroom and found me sitting on the bed going through the contents of a suitcase and she saw I was a bit emotional. She sat beside me, sympathetic but thankfully not speaking. There were papers and letters but nothing intimate (a typed copy of Magee's Poem I noticed – I wondered if it had helped Mrs Anderson in her loneliness) – and a few objects like a watch and binoculars, and she guessed it was Peter's stuff; Mrs Anderson had packed it together and written my name in felt-tip on the suitcase lid. I was looking for the Diaries. I knew he wrote a lot, not day by day, but more a journal in an exercise book, just jotted down when he wanted to preserve some fact or memory or idea – he was very intense and emotional about some things. I remember he wrote pages when his father died as he analysed his reactions. But I never read it, though of course I had opportunity as we shared a room; that was a deliberate decision on my part to give him a space not occupied by me. The last book, the one he had been using at Hawkinge, I had scrupulously not opened when I handed over his stuff at the funeral. But there were no journals in the suitcase, nor anywhere else in the flat. I felt cheated – I wanted to be close again to the mind that was Peter's, the bit we hadn't shared, and Mrs Anderson was robbing me, she had destroyed them. And of course she must have read them first.

'I never understood why he meant so much to you,' Elaine said. 'Were you.. did you.. you know, do sex? Were you really lovers?' She was hesitant; I guess she'd wondered before, but never felt able to ask. 'No!' I said. 'Never entered my thoughts. I had his mind, I certainly didn't want anything physical. We could joke about that sort of thing, boys discuss it, at that age, but it never led to anything with him or anyone else, I'd have hated it.' 'I wonder if he felt the same?' mused Elaine. I didn't answer; I didn't want to think about it. My Peter, as I wanted to remember him, in the last year of our eight years together (surely the most formative years of all, the developing years) was the joyous airman who *'... danced the skies on laughter-silvered wings ...'* and *'wheeled and soared and swung high in the sun-lit silence.'*

But Elaine had set me thinking nonetheless: could Peter have wanted a different relationship? And had he admitted it, even fantasised about it, in his Journals? And had his mother read that and destroyed them to protect his name from the world and from me? But if you think about it, she couldn't know if I'd read them or not, especially the last one he'd written at Hawkinge, which I handed over to her with his kit. If so, was the legacy a sort of apology, even an act of propitiation? Most of all, I wondered if I minded, or would have minded if I'd found out while he was still alive. He never locked the books away, so he was taking a chance I was too honourable to peep. Here is another thought: did he *want* me to read them? It might have destroyed a friendship though I don't think so, but for him it might have completed it. When we got back home I rang the solicitor and asked if there were any other effects anywhere else – papers left at his office for example? Of course the answer was no.

Magee talks of the *'untrespassed sanctity of space'*, and that doesn't only apply to soaring into the sunlit clouds: can't it also mean the *private* space that lovers share, from which outsiders are excluded? I believe I shared it with my friend Peter and his death diminished me. It occurs to me that I have written no poetry since.

---ooOoo---

MY AUNT PADDY

Britta von Zweigbergk

It was 1973 when I first arrived as a new art therapist at Bexley Hospital, a large psychiatric institution on the edge of Dartford Heath in Kent. I was initially surprised at my feelings of familiarity – it was not quite like working in a home from home, but I nevertheless felt comfortable and at ease.

In my little office – a glorified cupboard in many people's eyes – the garden and the general daily sounds of the hospital came across to me as a tangle of noise. There were some human voices but also there was the clatter and hum that emanated from the large kitchens and the noise of the porters' trolleys trundling along the corridors. These were a veritable labyrinth for newcomers like myself, who might feel as if they could be lost for ever in a maze of long and seemingly identical passages. In time I came to see the Art Therapy Department as somehow being at the centre of it all – the beating heart from which life and feeling and individuality still throbbed.

But then, on reflection, I wondered about my arrival into an unexpectedly rewarding working life, although it was only part-time while my children were still at school. It was a life I had not really planned for but to which I had responded immediately and unerringly, as doors and opportunities opened up to me and I stepped into a world of lost souls.

All of this might have had something to do with an earlier childhood memory – that of my Aunt Paddy in her room next to mine, and the sound of her continuous dialogue with herself and the world in general, throughout the night, rising and falling, the sound of laughter and secret jokes. That secret world that had been so enigmatic to me as a child was now all around me, echoing in the corridors, in the stairwells, the grounds and the summerhouses, and was even discernable in the wind.

Aunt Paddy had been part of my life ever since I could remember. My earliest recollection of her presence had been when I was a tiny child in North Muskham, when she had come to visit my mother, one of her younger sisters, and, trying uncharacteristically to be helpful, had buttered a slice of bread for me and spread Marmite on so thickly that it hurt my mouth.

Small children seem to be very accepting of strangeness, and I recognised her resemblance to my mother and other aunts in her naturally arched eyebrows and inflections of voice.

I was, I think, a little in awe of the way she differed from other significant adults in my life at that time: her way of walking and talking, particularly to herself, sometimes speaking in sharp little bursts of acrid and accusatory sound.

We were destined to live together during periods of my childhood from 1945 to 1947, 1950 to 1952, and 1958 to 1960. My maternal grandmother's teeming middle-floor flat (in 134 Elgin Avenue, Maida Vale, London W9) was the melting pot, the operational centre to which members of her large family regularly returned. Universally called 'Nan', she directed post-war life as best she could.

With my younger brother, my cousin, and myself, sharing one bedroom , we were next door to Paddy and her mutterings and strange rituals were a source of curiosity and wonder for us. Why for instance did she cover the radio at night, bless the countless pairs of shoes in her room, save glass jars, and believe she could recharge batteries?

A relationship evolved. We were known collectively as 'the brats' and tended to live up to her name for us. Giggling and teasing, tapping at her window or knocking at her door, we were, at various times, rewarded with shouts and bursts of anger. The possible danger of such situations – of being unexpectedly caught, for instance – was gloriously exciting to our young senses.

If, as happened in a crowded flat, we passed one another in the passage, her only acknowledgement of our presence was to hold the blanket round her more tightly than ever and press against the wall as if to eliminate any chance at all of our brushing accidentally against her, her blackened cup held aloft as she made her way to the kitchen for a further top-up of someone else's tea.

Even in the years that followed, when we lived elsewhere, 134 Elgin Avenue was regularly visited. But Paddy wasn't always there. There were long periods when she was 'away', variously and mysteriously described by my grandmother, mother and aunts as 'not well' or even more intriguingly as 'not herself'. Who, we wondered, was her real self and who was the self that took her place?

Eventually, I came to realise that at such times she was an in-patient at institutions such as Banstead and Horton Hospital, on the edge of windblown heathlands, with water towers against the sky proclaiming their separate and self-sufficient existence.

Although she spent long periods of time in such places and was adept at managing the currency of tea and cigarettes and the constant challenge of finding enough money to purchase both, she yearned for the outside world and being 'free' – back in her old stamping ground of West London.

Able to be clear, convincing, and articulate, when the occasion demanded it, she was discharged on occasions, usually with the repeated verbal intentions of 'looking after my mother' and promising to take the anti-psychotic medications such as Largactil, that had become available in the 50's and 60's, enabling those like herself who had been incarcerated for long periods in places like Banstead, to be considered for discharge. The great move back to the 'community' had begun.

Looking after Nan never seemed to happen. It was invariably the other way round. And it was the same, of course, with the taking of the prescribed medication. It was only a matter of time before the inevitable relapse. Paranoid schizophrenia, having arrived in her twenties, was not going to disappear or fade into the background. On the contrary, it remained, waiting for its end, and had died out by 1965. By the time the early 70's had arrived, my brother and cousin had moved out and there were just my mother and Paddy living together, not always harmoniously.

Life was not easy with my aunt as co-tenant. Possessed of a complete disregard for any housework and indeed of paying her way, life was a constant battle to make ends meet, since, in asking her to contribute to the rent and general living expenses was to no avail of course. One tried to coexist and remain hygienic.

The only way to begin to do this was to keep essentials like pans, cups, plates, cutlery, etc. separately and not in the shared kitchen. So, making a sandwich or cooking anything entailed making journeys along the passage with boxes and bags containing the required utensils. It took time and organisation and was frequently exhausting, infuriating, and demoralising for my mother.

The prevailing social culture at that time, where mental illness was concerned, was still stigma and shame. This dictated the way life would be for my mother, who was less garrulous and sociable than Nan. Extended social visits were not encouraged and did not take place. It was not actually passwords and the current code at the front door, visits were limited to close family. There was a certain melancholy and tragedy in this. One felt closed off and separate from the main stream of life, an ethos that could never be conducive to contentment.

For my part, my relationship with Paddy was a mixture of affection and exasperation in more or less equal measures. I supported the status quo, visited regularly, and frequently helped where I could. I knocked on my aunt's door and carried out shouted conversations. I attempted to keep the peace and shopped for both of them and, for a while, shared their closed off melancholy little world.

By the mid-70's the situation had become impossible and it was only a matter of time before my aunt was 'sectioned' and taken into hospital again. I had to set the wheels into motion and perform the painful task of taking her into Horton on my arm. As we stepped out of the ambulance and saw the hospital buildings and grounds in front of us, it felt like the ultimate betrayal.

    Aunt Paddy remained for the rest of her life in Horton Hospital, the sister hospital to Bexley. Each time I visited her with my mother, there was a disturbing sense of déjà vu in the replication of long corridors.

    I remained as art therapist at Bexley, staying until the department closed in 1996 with the hospital itself following suit in 2001. It seemed I was destined always to walk among lost souls, my aunt Paddy being the first and most memorable.

---ooOoo---

ABOUT THE AUTHORS

COLIN BIDDLE was born in London in1940. In 1958 he went to sea as a qualified radio officer and was at sea for 5 years. Then he worked in Australia and in 1966 moved to Hong Kong. He had 3 short stories accepted by a Christchurch daily newspaper. His novel Deadly Misunderstanding was published by Robert Hale. Woman's Realm printed a short story and he won a short story competition organised by a Hong Kong English newspaper. He returned to England in 1991.

BOB BROWN had a career in telecommunications for 30 years until, as a consequence of a life-transforming experience, he changed direction to study complementary & holistic health. Since 2006 he has practiced the healing art of Reiki as a therapist and subsequently as a teacher based in Folkestone. His work also includes meditation and mindfulness breathing practices for self-healing and spiritual awareness. He is currently writing a book about applying the principles of holistic healing to serious illness.

LIZ BROWN is a newcomer to short story writing, having written many local and human interest magazine articles. She is also a qualified Graphologist (www.graphologist-london.com). Previously she had a career in finance as a Chartered Accountant.

HELEN DERRY was an English teacher for 28 years. She retrained as a lawyer and practised family law for 10 years. She is married and has three children and ten grandchildren. She enjoys watercolour painting, Bridge, sailing, high mountain walking, and travelling all over the world. She started writing when she retired, mainly short stories

ANGELA GUIDOLIN was born in Italy in 1968. She is married and has a child. After graduating in Venice, she lived and worked in London and Lille (France), before moving back to Italy for a few years. She currently resides in Folkestone and divides her time between writing and taking care of her family. Her master degree in Business Economics has not changed her passion for literature, philosophy, spirituality and the desire to explore the human soul. She is interested in how new technologies can affect the meaning of being human.

MARGARET HARLAND-SUDDES came down to Folkestone from Durham 36 years ago with a husband, two children and qualifications from Durham University, to take up a post as founding head of Palmarsh C.P. School which she held for 20 years before taking early retirement. She has had a lifelong interest in Art and Creative Writing (prose and poetry) as well as writing and producing school plays and musicals

CHRIS HOLT is a recent resident of Folkestone. He has worked as a teacher in Devon and Australia, and as an administrator, broadcaster and field ecologist in Zimbabwe. He has written two novels and is working on his third. He has also published a volume of short stories.

HELEN HUDGELL has lived in Kent for most of her life. She was a teacher and now is not. She is enthusiastic about many things but is expert at nothing. She enjoys dabbling in a variety of pursuits with limited success. Her favourite possession is her collection of dictionaries. Her greatest hope is that one day she will understand why Jane Austen is so popular.

BRIONY KAPOOR grew up on Romney Marsh, was at school in Suffolk, and at University in Newcastle. She owned an art gallery in Central London before settling for many years in India with her husband, a distinguished academic. She returned to build her own house from where she set up the IMOS Foundation, an arts charity.

KATE LOCKWOOD JEFFORD, originally from Cardiff, has lived and worked in London (in the NHS since 1978, and since 2007has divided her time between London & Folkestone and is now finally back at the coast .She has always written, previously mainly for stage and theatre, but since completing a Guardian-University of East Anglia Creative Writing course in 2012, has focussed more on writing short stories, with ideas for a novel on the back-burner .Winner of the H G Wells Grand Short Story Prize in 2013, she was shortlisted for Chapter One Promotions International Short Story Competition in 2013, with a story to be published in the Chapter One Anthology in 2014. She's also had stories shortlisted for the Asham Prize 2012, and long listed for the Fish Short Story Prize, 2013.

MARTIN POSNETT was born in Birkenhead before moving across the Pennine way to Hull. His journey to Folkestone has included time as a ship's rigger, pig farmer, Welsh Guardsman, Actor, Director, and Teacher. He finally found the thing he loves to do most: he now teaches singing and has a thriving vocal studio based in the Creative Quarter of Folkestone.

PETER SHARPE studied at the Harvey Grammar School Folkestone and the University of Liverpool. He now lives and works in Maidstone. He enjoys writing in his spare time and particularly enjoys the works of James Joyce, Thomas Pynchon and Jorge Luis Borges. This is his first published work.

MICHELE SHELDON is a journalist and lives in Folkestone.

JACQUELINE SUMMER teaches Creative Writing (and art) for Kent Adult Education Service. She was a professional storyteller working with children and adults for 5 years from 2004. She mainly writes for pleasure and therapeutic purposes. Her poetry is published and exhibited alongside her art work. Jacqueline has had one of her plays performed.

JOHN SUSSAMS was educated at King Edward VII School, Sheffield, and Gonville & Caius College, Cambridge, reading Modern Languages. He has been a writer, off and on, during the whole of his working life in industry and as a management consultant, having published five technical books and numerous articles. After taking early retirement he moved to Folkestone in 1994 and has concentrated on painting and on creative writing. He has published three novels and a number of short stories.

ALEXANDER TULLOCH is a retired Senior Lecturer in Russian and Spanish. He worked with the MoD for many years and was latterly responsible for training interpreters in specialist reserve units. He has published translations of some of the classics in Spanish and Russian literature as well as several books of his own, including two on Liverpool, two on Kent and one on the origin of everyday words in English. He is a Fellow of the Chartered Institute of Linguists.

MIKE UMBERS read English at Trinity Hall, Cambridge, then unexpectedly became a career Soldier. He was posted to Hythe in 1983 and developed an interest in local history, so edited (i.e. wrote!) the Civic Society Newsletter for ten years and produced a commemorative book on Saltwood in 2007. He now contributes regular historical articles for the St Leonard's Church Parish Review. He is currently working on an Anthology of historical sketches about Hythe.

BRITTA VON ZWEIGBERGK lived in the Folkestone area in her teens and was a part time and then full time student at Folkestone Art School for a number of years. She became interested in art therapy and worked as an art therapist for over 40 years with the NHS. She has always been a working artist in a small way and has retained a love of writing . She is a published author and over the years has developed a keen interest in Social History , particularly the history of Asylums.